"What do you mean? I don't understand." *Please let it be a mistake.* **She couldn't spend her holiday with Harvey. They might actually kill each other.**

"We'll be working together for a couple of weeks," he said in confirmation, as if in no way concerned.

"You have got to be kidding me."

"I'm afraid not," Harvey said, starting the ignition. Then, leaning close, he added, "Love me or hate me, you're kind of stuck with me for a while."

Her lovely fortnight of sun and surgery, of giving something back to her Fijian counterparts before returning to her job in New Zealand refreshed and reinvigorated, dissolved before her eyes. Oh, she'd stick it out. If he could put up with her, she would put up with him.

But two weeks working with her professional rival? Two weeks trapped on an island with a man she knew intimately? Two weeks reminded of that incredible night in his bed when she hadn't had so much as a chaste peck on the cheek since...?

It sounded more like a prison sentence than a holiday.

Dear Reader,

There's something magical and so romantic about a holiday fling. So when I trapped love-hate rivals Della and Harvey together on one of the Fijian islands, I knew they would struggle to resist each other. But holidays don't last forever, even working holidays. I hope you enjoy reading *Forbidden Fiji Nights with Her Rival* to find out if Della and Harvey can turn a fling into forever.

Love,

JC x

FORBIDDEN FIJI NIGHTS WITH HER RIVAL

JC HARROWAY

Harlequin

MEDICAL ROMANCE

Harlequin®
MEDICAL
ROMANCE

Recycling programs
for this product may
not exist in your area.

ISBN-13: 978-1-335-94266-1

Forbidden Fiji Nights with Her Rival

Harlequin Enterprises ULC
22 Adelaide St. West, 41st Floor
Toronto, Ontario M5H 4E3, Canada
www.Harlequin.com

Printed in U.S.A.

Lifelong romance addict **JC Harroway** took a break from her career as a junior doctor to raise a family and found her calling as a Harlequin author instead. She now lives in New Zealand and finds that writing feeds her very real obsession with happy endings and the endorphin rush they create. You can follow her at jcharroway.com and on Facebook, X and Instagram.

Books by JC Harroway

Harlequin Medical Romance

A Sydney Central Reunion

Phoebe's Baby Bombshell

Buenos Aires Docs

Secretly Dating the Baby Doc

Gulf Harbour ER

Tempted by the Rebel Surgeon
Breaking the Single Mom's Rules

Forbidden Fling with Dr. Right
How to Resist the Single Dad
Her Secret Valentine's Baby
Nurse's Secret Royal Fling

Visit the Author Profile page
at Harlequin.com for more titles.

To writer friends, especially the CC ladies

CHAPTER ONE

ENTERING THE ARRIVAL hall of Fiji's Nadi Airport, Della Wilton sighed happily. Despite coming for a working holiday, the minute she'd stepped from the plane's metal staircase onto the sun-baked tarmac, her problems had dissolved, one by one.

Della hefted her overstuffed suitcase onto the airport luggage trolley, stubbing her toe in the process. She winced in pain, but not even a fractured digit could dispel her buoyant mood. Two whole weeks of sun, seminars and pro bono surgery at Pacific Health Hospital on Fiji's main island, Viti Levu. Just the boost she needed after the stagnation of the past three and a half years since her divorce.

With her cases secured, Della sought out the exit, already dreaming of snorkelling the coral reefs of the clear, pristine waters and lounging in a hammock strung between two coconut palms. She knew from previous family holidays and, more recently, her ill-fated honeymoon marking the start of her three-year marriage that there was a taxi rank outside. But she'd barely taken two steps in that direction when her laden trolley jammed to a halt, the wheels locking. Della grunted, momentarily winded from her midsection colliding with the handle bar. Trust her to choose the duff trolley. She reversed, hoping to free the sticky wheels, to no avail.

Another jerking halt sent her carry-on case tumbling to the floor with a loud clatter. Della bent to retrieve it. The back of her neck was already clammy from the heat and humidity and the battle with her luggage. Frazzled, she straightened. Came face-to-face with the last person in the world she expected to see in Fiji: Harvey Ward.

'Della...' he drawled, an amused smile tugging at his sexy mouth. He eyed her big case suspiciously, as if it was full of sex toys, chocolate and tequila—the sad single woman's survival kit. 'Hasn't anyone ever explained the principle of travelling light?'

Before Della could articulate a single stunned word in reply, Harvey swooped in and pressed a kiss to her cheek. Della gaped, disorientated, speechless and instantly and inconveniently turned on by the foreign contact, which zapped her nerve endings as if she'd been pleasantly electrocuted. He'd never done that before. Their usual form of greeting was a reluctant nod of acknowledgement or a terse *hello*.

'What on Earth are *you* doing here?' she snapped, abandoning the polite indifference she usually produced when addressing this man— not quite a friend, although they'd known each other for years. Not a full-blown enemy, although, as the more experienced trauma surgeon, he *had* stolen Della's dream job in Melbourne. And definitely not a lover; apart from that one reckless night after the granting of her divorce order three years ago, when, feeling rejected and embarrassed, she'd drunk too much rosé and had temporarily lost her mind.

On cue, Della's body helpfully recalled every detail of how it felt to be naked in his strong arms. They'd had sex one time, and she still couldn't forget.

'It's good to see you, too.' Harvey laughed with infuriating composure, by-passing Della to select a new trolley, one that appeared to have perfectly behaved wheels.

Hateful man was good at *everything*. How dare he look so cool, relaxed, and indecently arousing in his casual linen shorts and polo shirt which showed off his light tan and lean, athletic build, when Della felt decidedly in need of another shower, preferably a cold one.

'I'm here to pick you up,' he stated simply.

Della pushed her damp, frizzy hair back from her flustered face, her skin crawling with head-to-toe prickly heat. 'Oh, well, that explains everything,' she muttered, her stomach taking a disappointed dive. The last person she wanted to *bump into* on her holiday was her professional rival and personal nemesis, Harvey. Especially when he'd obviously come all the way from Australia to goad her and point out her failings, as usual.

'I heard that,' he said with an amused shrug, effortlessly transferring her suitcases from *her* wonky trolley to *his* better one. 'What...? Not pleased to see me?'

At his flippancy, Della pressed her lips together stubbornly. That was another thing that got under her skin—just like her older brother, Brody, Harvey's best friend, the man had a competitive streak a mile wide. Probably why Harvey was so at home with her family, an over-achieving clan of medics. Della's parents were GPs and Brody one of Australia's top renal surgeons. As the youngest sibling, Della had grown up scared that she'd never quite make the grade, a feeling that only intensified when self-assured, arrogant Harvey had been welcomed into the family as an honorary Wilton.

With both suitcases now perfectly balanced on the replacement trolley, Harvey shot Della a triumphant smile, commandeered the handle bar and began to stroll towards the exit, as if assured that she'd follow.

'So you're still bearing a grudge, I see,' he said, glancing over his broad shoulder, his stare brimming with the hint of challenge that never failed to raise Della's hackles.

Ever since Brody had first introduced them to Harvey—Della had been eighteen and about to leave for medical school—there'd been something about the newly qualified doctor, a hunger in his eyes, that had left Della mildly threatened. It was as if Harvey knew some big secret she was too stupid to see. She'd fancied him, of course, despite being in a relationship with her engineering student boyfriend. Harvey was a good-looking man. Even then, at twenty-three, before he'd become a surgeon, he'd possessed that air of supreme confidence. But only minutes into their first conversation, it had become glaringly obvious that they would never get along. Their mutual contempt had been instantaneous, their first impressions of each other terrible.

Brody had regaled Della with the tale of some poor woman Harvey had slept with the night before but wasn't going to call again. Harvey had merely shrugged, saying, "I told her it was nothing serious". Meanwhile, Della had been upset to leave her boyfriend and do long-distance, and Harvey had joined in with Brody's teasing, throwing out an insensitive "it probably won't last". Still dreamily in love at the time, Della had taken instant umbrage to Harvey's dismissive attitude to relationships. He'd acted as if the pursuit of love and commitment was beneath him and only for fools.

'I am not bearing a grudge,' Della said, hurrying after him, although at six-two he towered over her five-foot-six, his long stride giving him an unfair advantage. 'But I should point out that you *did* actually steal my job.'

She hated the bitter whine to her voice. Of course she was bearing a grudge. Technically, the position of head of trauma surgery at Melbourne Medical Centre wasn't *her* job. Technically, Harvey had just as much right to it as Della. But having already moved from her native Melbourne to Sydney for her ex-husband a couple of years earlier, and after the humiliation of her divorce, she'd desperately needed the professional win to boost her confidence. To lose a position to Harvey, of all people, especially after she'd slept with him, had been a bitter pill to swallow, leading Della to flee *across the ditch* to New Zealand for a consultant position in order to get away from Sydney and Ethan.

'Is it my fault that they wanted the best surgeon for the job?' he said with a wink. He passed through the automatic exit doors, where a blast of conditioned air bathed Della in his sexy masculine scent.

His casual comment nudged awake her highly evolved competitive streak. 'No, but it *is* your fault that you're an arrogant control freak.' She didn't notice he'd come to a halt until she'd collided with him, her breasts brushing his arm. She looked up, her face and her body on fire. He was too close and too tall and too… Harvey.

She stepped back, ignoring the playfulness in his dark eyes, because all she could see was the intense way he'd looked at her *that* night when he'd made her sob out his name.

'Come on, Della,' he cajoled, flashing that dazzlingly confident smile as if already certain of his powers to charm, 'it's been three years since the Melbourne job. Don't you think it's time to forgive me, to bury the proverbial hatchet, preferably somewhere other than in my skull?'

'If only…' Della muttered, fuming. She reached for the trolley, yanking it away from his control. Just because he liked to be in the driving seat didn't mean he could commandeer *her*. She caught another waft of his subtle cologne, the fresh laundry scent of his clothes and the warmth of his body, and fought the uninvited and intimate memories of that one night.

Sleeping with him had served to remind her that, despite being in her mid-thirties, she'd still been an attractive woman. Who better than love 'em and leave 'em bachelor Harvey to show her a life-affirming good time free of any strings? Because when it came to sex, he'd had plenty of practice. She'd heard the stories from Brody.

'Why *are* you here?' she demanded, coming to a defiant halt. 'Not at the airport, manhandling my cases, but here in Fiji?' More importantly, why had she meekly followed him outside when she'd always done her best to steer clear? From that first disastrous meeting, they'd rarely seen eye to eye, instead bickering like a long-suffering married couple. Harvey liked nothing better than to goad both Della and every boyfriend she'd ever brought to a family event, and Della could never seem to help rolling her eyes at his latest sexploits, affronted by his attitude towards commitment on behalf of all women.

'I was invited here by Dr Tora,' he said with a casual shrug, 'head of surgery at Pacific Health. Didn't they tell you?' He took a set of car keys from his pocket and dangled them from one long, elegant and capable finger, his easy smile further fuelling her irritation.

'Tell me what?' Della's blood chilled a few degrees, despite the hot tropical air clinging to her skin. Her voice carried a whiny pleading quality that hurt her eardrums. But whenever Harvey was around, she felt wrong-footed. Unstable. On her guard. But she couldn't show any weakness.

'That like you, I'm here to run a few seminars and have offered my surgical skills pro bono.' He dropped the bombshell and sauntered towards a nearby open-top Jeep with the hospital's name emblazoned on the door.

The hairs on the back of her neck rose. Floundering, *again*, Della hurried after him with her trolley. 'What do you mean? I don't understand.' *Please let it be a mistake.* She couldn't spend her holiday with Harvey. They might actually kill each other.

'We'll be working together for a couple of weeks,' he said in confirmation, as if in no way concerned. Effortlessly, he lifted her cases into the back of the Jeep, parked the empty trolley and walked to the driver's side, pulling his sunglasses from where he'd tucked them into the neck of his shirt.

Della wobbled on her feet, disoriented and overheated as if she was spinning inside a tumble dryer. Working together? They'd never done that before. It would be a disaster. She'd have to see him every day at the hospital with no hope of avoiding his arrogant swagger or his potent sex appeal? How was *that* fair?

'You have got to be kidding me,' she muttered, a string of swear words running through her head as she yanked open the passenger door and reluctantly climbed inside the Jeep.

'I'm afraid not,' Harvey said, starting the ignition and then leaning close to add, 'Love me or hate me, you're kind of stuck with me for a while.'

Oh, how easily they slipped into their respective roles, their game of one-upmanship, even here in beautiful Fiji. But as usual, Della felt one step behind. 'No, you're stuck with *me*,' she snapped childishly, crossing her arms and staring out of the window as Harvey chuckled and pulled out of the parking space, heading for the airport exit.

Della's lovely fortnight of sun and surgery, of giving something back to her Fijian counterparts before returning to her job in New Zealand refreshed and reinvigorated, dissolved before her eyes. Oh, she'd stick it out—she'd never allow Harvey Ward, of all people, to chase her off. If he could put up with her, she would put up with him.

But two weeks working with her professional rival? Two weeks trapped on an island with a man she knew intimately? Two weeks reminded of that incredible night in his bed when she hadn't had so much as a chaste peck on the cheek since…?

It sounded more like a prison sentence than a holiday.

CHAPTER TWO

A SOLID THIRTY MINUTES. That's how long it had taken Harvey to calm down after the brief but silent car journey to the hospital with Della. Even now, after a close shave, a cold shower and a fresh shirt and chinos, he could still feel the itch of her under his skin. The infuriating woman needled him like no other and always had. Of course, she was also mind-blowingly sexy.

'…and this is our emergency department, as you know,' said Dr Tora, Pacific Health Hospital's clinical chief of surgery, drawing Harvey away from memories of that one night three years ago when, after socialising with her family, Della had shocked him with a goodbye kiss to the cheek that had turned…explosive. As explosive as the back-and-forth bickering that had always been their main form of communication.

Forcing his head back into the game, Harvey waved hello to a few of the ED staff he recognised from his previous visits. He was proud to continue his support of this hospital. The last thing he needed was for his long-standing discord with Della to tarnish the reputation he'd built over the years.

Just then, Dr Tora's pager sounded. The older man silenced it and read the display. 'Oh dear. I'm afraid I have to go. Can I entrust Dr Wilton's security pass to you? I'm sure she'll be here soon.'

'Of course.' Harvey took the lanyard as if it were a live snake and slipped it into his pocket. Where was Della? His entire reason for meeting her at the airport was to try and mitigate any awkwardness. Since that night they'd had sex, they'd seen each other maybe six times, always in the presence of the other Wiltons. Instead, she'd fried his brain with that sexy little sundress she'd been wearing. Her blond hair was longer that the last time he'd seen her, the cut somehow softer so it fell in waves around her stunning heart-shaped face. But roaring attraction aside, they'd slipped so effortlessly into their respective roles—hers of barely concealed annoyance and his goading out those flashes of fire from her blue eyes—that clearing the air before they headed to the hospital had completely fled his mind. Images of her naked on top of him and under him, her defiant stare judging him even as she cried out in pleasure, had flashed before his eyes. They'd never once talked about that night, simply pretended that it hadn't happened. But as he'd said to her in the car, like it or not, they were stuck with each other. They'd need to find some way of putting all of that aside to work together. Harvey winced, braced for a very long fortnight.

A rushed patter of feet caused him and Dr Tora to turn around. Out of breath, Della appeared. Still flustered. Still scowling at Harvey. Still sexy as hell. Harvey groaned silently, calling to mind how she always looked at him as if he was something unsavoury she'd found on the bottom of her shoe to manage the constant temptation.

'Sorry I'm late,' she said, addressing Dr Tora and completely ignoring Harvey. 'I got a little lost.' She laced her lovely smile with apology as she stuck out her hand. 'I'm Della Wilton from Auckland's Harbour Hospital. Thank you so much for having me here at Pacific Health.'

Like Harvey, Della had obviously showered and changed since he'd dropped her at the staff bungalows an hour ago. She smelled fantastic, like an ocean breeze, her simple sleeveless dress doing nothing to hide her sensational body, not that Harvey needed a road map. He possessed an excellent memory, and he'd had nearly twenty years to study Della's abundant plus points.

'Bula, Dr Wilton,' Dr Tora said. 'I'm afraid you've just missed the tour of the surgical department, and I must excuse myself. I have an urgent referral patient to see. But I'll leave you in Dr Ward's capable hands. He knows his way around like a local after all these years.'

With a warm smile, Dr Tora departed, leaving Harvey and Della to what would no doubt be another polite and impersonal conversation, as was their norm.

'After all these years?' she asked, eyeing him suspiciously, as if he'd deliberately ruined her holiday with his presence. Her cheeks were flushed from rushing, the pale freckles on her nose a major distraction. He had intimate knowledge that they matched the ones across her shoulders and chest. Thinking about her freckles led to thinking about her naked, her gorgeous curves revealed for his greedy stare and hands. Her shockingly wild passion that, no matter how hard he tried, or how fiercely they argued, he just couldn't forget. They were like oil and water, incompatible but still flammable.

Harvey silently counted to five before opening his mouth in the hopes that he wouldn't say the wrong thing that would lead to another bickering match. The day they'd met, he'd still been grieving the death of his one and only girlfriend, Alice, sleeping around to numb the pain. Then, reeling from his instant and inconvenient attraction to his best friend's sister, he'd made some clumsy, thoughtless and cynical comment that Della and her long-distance boyfriend likely wouldn't survive them studying in different cities, in different states. Della had never forgiven him. Over the years, she took every opportunity to point out that, when it came to relationships, they wanted very different things, and her way was better.

'I come here every year,' he said, leading the way to the emergency department staff room. 'I usually run a few update seminars for our Fijian colleagues, do a few surgeries to help out.' It wasn't like he had a partner or family to holiday with, and he'd always preferred to keep busy.

'Of course you do,' she scoffed, her kissable mouth pursed with irritation. 'Why is it that you're everywhere I look, Harvey—invited to *my* family functions, working *my* job in Melbourne and now hijacking *my* holiday?'

'I could say that you followed me, Della,' he pointed out, his stare drawn to the elegant slope of her neck, a place he remembered the skin was soft and fragrant. 'It's not like I came to Fiji this year with the sole purpose of rattling your cage.'

'I wouldn't put it past you,' she muttered, walking off.

Harvey dragged in a deep breath. How would he survive two weeks in her company when they could barely make it through one conversation before she took umbrage or he goaded her? Should he remind *little miss high and mighty* how she'd used him for rebound sex three years ago, after her divorce?

Following, he caught up with her outside the occupied staff room where several nurses were taking a break. 'So, this is the ED staff room,' he said, biting his tongue for the sake of harmony. 'And this is the doctors' office.' Across the corridor, they found the office empty and stepped inside. 'Computer terminals, printers, photocopier, etc.' Harvey slipped his hand into his pocket and pulled out her security pass. 'Use this to log in to the computer and printer.'

She took it, her expression wary.

Harvey scanned his own pass over the digital display in pointless demonstration. Della was a consultant trauma surgeon in New Zealand's leading hospital. She was perfectly capable of figuring out how to use a photocopier. Enough procrastinating. Time to have that tricky personal conversation.

'So, how have you been?' he asked, shoving his hands in his trouser pockets to appear relaxed and non-threatening. Better to get the sex talk out of the way before they started work.

'Oh, you know…' she said, moving around the room, away from him, as she pretended to scrutinise the posters on the notice board. 'Still the same old Della—still divorced, still working in Auckland.'

She always did that when she felt threatened— pointed out what she considered to be her worst failings, as if saying them aloud first, before anyone else could, was a defence mechanism. Not that Harvey had been about to raise either of those touchy subjects. He wasn't stupid.

'Look, Della,' he said, pushing the office door closed to give them a bit of privacy. 'I collected you from the airport because I wanted to clear the air.' He stepped into her line of vision so she couldn't ignore him. 'I know we've never talked about that night, but it was just sex.'

Just sex. The kind that had forever altered his perception and awareness of this woman. For sixteen years he'd successfully fought his attraction to her, thinking of her only as the untouchable sister of his best friend, a feat for which he surely deserved some sort of gold medal.

'There's no need to allow it to interfere with us working together for the next two weeks,' he finished, keeping his stare locked with hers. Because to look at her body was to remember that night and the way it had lit some sort of primed fuse and changed everything. Since then, there was no ignoring Della, his only defence to keep reminding himself that she was a relationship person and he was the opposite.

'As if,' she scoffed, a telltale flush creeping up her neck. 'I'm a professional, and it wasn't *that* good.'

'Liar,' he said simply, daring her with his eyes to argue the point so he could bring up how they'd set the bed ablaze, how she'd come twice and left his place looking sexily satisfied, if a little dazed. But then she'd confessed he'd been her first since her marriage had broken down six months earlier. Thinking about how she'd used *good old Harvey* to get over her ex that night, his stomach twisted. He hadn't realised how much it had bothered him until the next day when he'd awoken with the scent of her perfume on his sheets. He'd wanted to call her so badly, he'd locked his phone in the filing cabinet at work.

But Della hadn't finished insulting him.

'Well, there's no need to worry that I'll tempt you to break your *one time and done* rule,' she said, her expression withering.

She'd always made it clear what she thought of Harvey's commitment avoidance, always judged him and stuck up for the women he slept with and looked at him as if he was some kind of dirt bag. Of course, she had no idea that keeping his brief relationships superficial was how Harvey dealt with the losses in his life. Both his mother and Alice had left him in their different ways, and he never wanted there to be a third woman who made him feel powerless. He was better off alone and in control.

Harvey shook his head in disbelief, her jibe predictable but no less offensive. 'I'm not worried, and I don't have a *one time and done* rule.' He almost wished he did. That way he absolutely wouldn't be thinking about sleeping with Della again.

And was it his fault that Della was a relationship person, and with the exception of Alice, he was a bit of a loner? Was it his fault they shared a competitive streak, that they were professionally similar but personally opposites? She'd grown up surrounded by the loving but boisterous Wilton family, whereas Harvey's mother had abandoned him when he was eight years old. Was it his fault that, over the years, Harvey had deliberately stayed single whereas Della had fallen in and out of love with several unworthy men who'd one by one broken her too-big heart?

'And yet you're forty-two and have never been in a relationship that lasts longer than a bottle of milk,' she said, that curl of contempt tugging at her gorgeous mouth.

'Why do you always do that?' he asked, once more questioning the wisdom of coming to Fiji as planned once he'd discovered from Brody that Della would also be there.

'Do what?' She put one hand on her hip as if

deliberately taunting him with her spectacular figure.

'Insinuate that my sex life bothers you?' He took a half step closer, his pulse accelerating as her pupils dilated, as if their bickering was a kind of verbal foreplay. 'Being sceptical about love isn't a crime, Della. And it didn't seem to matter when you needed a quick roll in the hay to celebrate the granting of your divorce order.'

She might despise his lifestyle, see him as some sort of threat because their views on commitment were so dissimilar, but she couldn't deny their rampant chemistry.

'It *doesn't* bother me,' she said, her breaths coming a little faster and her cheeks reddening. 'And don't act as if you hoped us sleeping together three years ago would be the start of something more. That's not your style.'

She was right. Just because they were trapped there together, he'd be a fool to act on this, a fool to do anything but ignore it as usual.

'So? You knew what you were getting into that night and wanted me anyway,' he pointed out. 'Perhaps because you needed a safe bet, and good old Harvey was available.' It was a low blow, but he couldn't stop himself from taunting her, not when she was acting so...holy. Not when she'd used him and never mentioned it again. Had she even given that night a second thought over the past three years?

Her mouth hung open and she blinked up at him, maybe searching for something cutting to say. But Harvey had already exposed too much. He didn't want her to know he'd been aware that he'd served a purpose that night. That her using him had stung. Maybe he could exact a little revenge now.

Stepping closer, he lowered his voice. 'Perhaps you like the idea of spending another night in my bed, Della. If that's the case, you only have to ask. For you, my bedroom door is always open.'

'Of course it is,' she muttered, triumph glittering in her wide stare. 'Same old Harvey. You never change.'

'Neither do your judgements,' he said, tempted to exaggerate stories of his past philandering for maximum effect. 'But as you've raised the subject of relationships, you obviously want me to ask. So, are *you* seeing anyone? Is husband-to-be number two waiting for you back in Auckland?'

Harvey clamped his runaway mouth shut. He didn't want to upset her any more than he already had just by being there. But a twist of envy gripped his gut. He shouldn't care if she was dating again. It was none of his business. All he needed to do was get through these two weeks in one piece.

Della raised her chin, her eyes dipping, but not before Harvey spied a flash of doubt. So that was *no* then. Hell…it would be so much easier for him if she was dating and therefore untouchable again.

'I've been busy…' she confirmed, glancing away. 'Moving countries, starting a new job, travelling home to Melbourne to visit my family every chance I get.'

Another dig about the Melbourne job… But now, fingers of unease slithered up Harvey's spine. Was she talking about the past three and a half years?

'So no dating at all since your divorce?' he pushed, the pitch of his voice changing to incredulous. Did that mean she hadn't slept with anyone else since she'd slept with *him*? Surely not. But now he was aflame with curiosity.

'My love life doesn't concern you,' she said primly, her stare bold.

Harvey saw red. 'Not even when you used me for sex, knowing that you were safe to walk away and never mention it again, despite the fact that we see each other all the time?' Now why had he said that? Why couldn't he have handed over her security pass, ignored how badly he wanted to kiss her and kept his mouth shut? Why was it these days, since that one hot night, he and Della always seemed to have some sort of unfinished business?

Her mouth agape, she blinked up at him, breathing hard.

His own heart rate thundering, his gaze dipped to the lovely curve of her lips. He knew how those lips tasted, recalled how they parted on breathy sighs. Had felt them against his skin as she'd cried out in passion. The metallic taste of fear coated his mouth. Forget the awkwardness; it wasn't their biggest problem. He wasn't going to survive these two weeks, fourteen long days, in Della's company without cracking and doing something stupid. Perhaps he should just kiss her now, suggest they sleep together again and get the sex out of their systems so they could go back to bickering over nothing.

Just then, as they faced each other, head-to-head, stares locked in defiance, there was a knock at the door. They stepped away from each other as Seema, one of the ED nurses, entered the room.

'Harvey, we've just had a walk-in casualty, and it looks bad—can you come?'

'Of course,' Harvey said, rushing to the trauma bay in the ED with Della at his heels. All the adrenaline he'd prepared for sparring with Della fuelled him now as he joined the man being wheeled on a stretcher into the resuscitation bay.

'His work colleagues literally carried him in,' Seema said about the patient, who was conscious and groaning in pain, his breathing harsh behind an oxygen mask. 'He fell from second-floor scaffolding, a drop of over twenty feet. His name is Warren.'

Harvey glanced at Della as he reached for a stethoscope. Their reckoning would have to wait. As if they were used to working together, she took up position opposite Harvey, on the other side of the patient, reaching for a second stethoscope, as the nurses cut away the man's clothing to expose his chest. Harvey noted his vital signs. His blood pressure was on the low side, his heart rate rapid but regular.

'He has an open fracture of the left humerus,' Della said, her eyes meeting Harvey's in silent communication.

Their casualty would be heading to theatre, but first they needed to eliminate anything more life-threatening than a broken arm.

'Any loss of consciousness or seizures?' Harvey asked Seema, testing the man's pupillary reflexes with a pen torch. They needed to exclude a head injury. Fortunately someone had fitted a neck brace to immobilise the man's cervical spine.

'No,' Seema said. 'One of the work colleagues who brought him in was on the ground and got to him pretty quickly.'

'I just need to examine you, Warren.' Harvey palpated the trachea above the breast bone before placing his stethoscope over the lung fields to listen to the breath sounds.

'He's got a pneumothorax on the left and tracheal deviation,' he told Della, knowing she would understand the urgency of the man's condition. In cases of tension pneumothorax, if they didn't drain out the escaped air from his chest and reinflate the collapsed lung, he could go into shock.

Della nodded, reaching for a sterile wide-bore cannula from the trolley at the head of the casualty. They needed to relieve the pressure on the heart by allowing the trapped air to escape before they could organise X-rays or they risked cardiac arrest.

'I think he might have a flail chest on this side,' Della said, adding to the list of problems. 'There's a lot of bruising of the chest wall and some surgical emphysema.' She peeled open the cannula as the blood pressure monitor emitted an ear-piercing alarm.

'His blood pressure is dropping. Let's decompress and then review,' he said to Della, who quickly swabbed the skin and inserted the needle into the man's chest cavity to allow the trapped air from the punctured lung to escape.

Harvey drew up some intravenous analgesia and, as the blood pressure rose, administered it via a cannula in the patient's arm. 'Warren. We think you might have some fractured ribs that have punctured the lung. We're going to organise some X-rays to be sure.'

'Let's get a chest drain kit ready, please,' Della said to Seema. 'And we need an urgent cross-match for blood transfusion.' She quickly labelled some blood vials and handed them to a porter, who would run them around to the haematology lab.

With the patient stabilised for now, Harvey and Della moved aside to talk, their personal grievances and the constant pull of attraction set aside.

'That humerus will need to be internally fixed,' Della said with a frown of concern, shifting to make room for the radiographer, who wheeled in the mobile X-ray machine.

'We might need to surgically stabilise the fractured ribs, too,' Harvey said, his mind racing through the worst-case scenarios for the patient. Often, a flail segment, an area of ribs fractured in more than one place, was treated with mechanical ventilation and analgesia, but in some instances, surgery was required, especially if there were other complications like chest wall damage, haemorrhage or rib dislocations.

Della nodded in agreement. 'I'll call the anaesthetist and theatre. Either way, he'll need to be admitted to ICU.'

'And I'll speak to Warren's next of kin and consent him for surgery,' Harvey said, impressed with the way they'd forgotten their personal differences and their competitive natures and worked together for the first time.

'I didn't expect to operate on our first day.' She looked up at him, a flicker of surprise and respect shining in her eyes. 'Do you want the humerus or the chest?'

'Let's figure it out together when we get to theatre,' he said, confident that Della and he could set aside everything else when it came to their work.

'Sounds like a plan,' she said, her expression registering relief.

Before they found themselves trapped together in Fiji, he'd have been convinced they would squabble over the decision or over who was the better surgeon. But when it came to the safety of their patient, there was no room for ego, despite how he'd teased her earlier at the airport.

As they set about their different tasks, putting their patient first, Harvey wondered how long their enforced truce would last. Their sexual chemistry was obviously going nowhere. They would need to revisit the conversation on how best to manage it, providing they could tolerate each other long enough to talk.

As predicted, it was going to be the longest fortnight of Harvey's life.

CHAPTER THREE

LATER THAT NIGHT, after a full afternoon of surgery, Della took her frosty glass of beer from the barman and headed outside. Savu's, a beach bar a short walk from the hospital, had a handful of tables set on the sand. What better way to unwind than watching the stunning Fijian sun set. After her eventful and unexpected first day, she desperately needed time to put everything into perspective. Like how she'd almost kissed Harvey Ward earlier in the emergency department doctors' office…

What the hell had she been thinking? She'd had her 'roll in the hay', as he'd put it. The shameful memory of his hurt expression returned. He'd accused her of using him for sex that night, which she probably had on some level. But surely Harvey wouldn't have cared, would he? The man was a walking one-night stand. But maybe tomorrow, she should apologise.

Della stepped outside and instantly spied Harvey sitting alone at one of the tables near the water's edge. Her stomach swooped at the sight of him—long legs stretched out as he relaxed, his fingers casually gripping a beer bottle, his gaze trained on the ocean view. Della froze, her first instinct to forget her apology and avoid him, as usual. She could duck back inside the bar, down her beer and scurry home to her accommodation without having to analyse just how badly she still wanted the annoyingly arrogant man, despite the fact she had to work with him for the next two weeks and he still knew how to push all of her buttons.

For you, my bedroom door is always open... Right—for her and every other single woman on the planet.

As if he'd heard her scoff, he turned, and their eyes met. Della's body flushed from head to toe with that familiar jolt of attraction. Dammit, she couldn't run away now that he'd seen her, but nor did she particularly want to talk to him. If they somehow managed a conversation without bickering or hurling insults, she might feel compelled to admit that she'd found new respect for him as a doctor.

They'd spent hours in theatre with their fall casualty, internally fixing the man's fractured humerus and multiple rib fractures. To her confusion, she'd learned that Harvey was far from arrogant in the OR. When it came to surgery, he was meticulously thorough. He'd even shown humility, asking for her preferred surgical technique when it came to wiring versus plating of rib fractures.

Harvey casually raised his hand, beckoning her to join him, an easy, perfectly amicable smile tugging at that delicious mouth of his. How could he be so unaffected by her when she was all over the place? Hot with resentment that, when it came to getting over that night they'd slept together, Harvey had easily cruised into first place, leaving Della second best, she begrudgingly crossed the sand in his direction. Maybe she was simply stressed out by the idea of having him around 24-7. They'd spent more one-on-one time together today than they'd spent in the preceding nineteen years of their strained relationship. Normally, they tolerated each other for an evening maximum, and the social contact was always diluted by the presence of the other Wiltons.

As she arrived at his table, Harvey stood, pulling out the second chair. 'Great minds think alike.'

His smile, the way he swept his gaze over her, tripled her pulse rate. Why was he always so comfortable in his skin? Why did everything he did and said annoy her, so she came out fighting? Why did he have to go and show her what an all-round good guy he was, regularly donating his time and expertise here in Fiji? It was seriously messing with those preconceived assumptions she'd always clung to in order to keep Harvey in a nice, neat box.

'Yes, that was quite the first day.' Della sat and took a hasty sip of her drink, struggling anew with the surge of undeniable attraction. 'I needed to unwind.' Fat chance of that now…

'No place better than Savu's.' He smiled and raised his bottle in a toast. 'To beautiful Fijian nights.'

See, there he went again, being…nice. Della reluctantly clinked her glass to his bottle, her stomach fluttering as his stare held hers while he took a long, lazy swallow. He was so sexy, it wasn't fair. Perhaps she should sleep with him again and get it out of her system. Three years without sex really was too long—maybe when she returned to New Zealand, she should seriously consider dating again.

Jealous that she couldn't feel as unaffected by him as he appeared by her, Della scrabbled around for something to say that wasn't *I'd like to take you up on your offer and push open that bedroom door.*

'I checked on our fall patient before I left the hospital,' she said instead. 'He's stable and comfortable on ICU.'

'I checked too.' Harvey's eyes narrowed a fraction, that smug hint of amusement touching his lips, telling Della he could easily read her mind and sense her discomfort. 'But do you really want to talk shop when we could be enjoying the sunset?'

He inclined his head towards the pink-orange streaks in the sky, which deeply contrasted with the blackening sea and the patch of white sand illuminated by the lights strung overhead from the rear of the bar. Della pressed her lips together defiantly. If they couldn't talk about work, what the hell were they going to discuss? Maybe simply getting physical again was the *only* answer.

'How's Brody?' she asked, chugging another gulp of her drink, irritated by how effortlessly he could turn her on. Yes, talking about her family would smother the flames of their chemistry. Especially when it reminded her that, if not for Harvey, she would be working in Melbourne, where she belonged.

'Don't you know?' he asked, that mocking little half smile keeping her on her guard. 'He's *your* brother.'

'But you see more of him than I do,' she whined, dragging her stare away from the open neck of his shirt to where she knew his chest and torso was an anatomist's dream of sun-bronzed skin and delineated muscle. She offered him a tight smile. 'Since you stole my Melbourne job.'

She really needed to let this feud go; it was childish. And if he hadn't hijacked the lovely working holiday she'd planned, if he hadn't goaded her into talk of their sex lives, if she hadn't almost kissed him again, maybe she could have.

'Brody is good,' Harvey said with a small sigh. 'He and Amy are busy with work, but looking forward to baby Jack's naming day celebration.'

Della nodded, her heart full of longing to see her baby nephew again. She didn't need to ask if Harvey was invited to the Wilton family gathering in a month's time. He was invited to most events. Like she'd pointed out earlier, there was no escaping him.

'Look, Della, about the job…' he continued, turning serious. 'I wanted to explain. I don't know if Brody mentioned it, but my dad hasn't been well these past couple of years. I applied for that position because I really needed to stay in Melbourne. I'm all the family he has.'

Stunned by his vulnerable admission, Della shook her head in confusion. 'I didn't know. Brody never mentioned it. What's wrong with Bill?' She knew Harvey's parents were divorced and that he was close to his father. But Harvey had never opened up to her before, nor vice versa, as if they'd made an unspoken pact to keep each other at arm's length. Brody was adamant his friend had *hidden depths*, but until this very moment, she'd always doubted their existence.

'He's fine.' Harvey shrugged, clearly worried about Bill Ward but downplaying it. 'He's been diagnosed with multiple sclerosis,' he continued, his voice emotionless but his fingers picking at the corner of the beer label.

Shocked, her face heating because of how petulantly she'd acted when she hadn't known the full story, Della's throat tightened. Poor Bill. Harvey's dad was often included in family get-togethers at Christmas or on Australia Day. Della liked him a lot.

'I'm so sorry to hear that, Harvey.' Before she'd even realised she'd moved, Della found her hand resting on Harvey's warm, muscular forearm. Her comforting gesture spread tingles up her own arm. She pulled her hand away. Touching him was a no-no if she hoped to keep their sexual chemistry under control. And if Harvey could successfully ignore it, so could she.

'You must be worried about him,' she pushed, instinct telling her that control freak Harvey was probably in denial. Not that she could blame him. No one wanted to think of their parents ageing or becoming sick.

Harvey shrugged, pulling a deep drag of beer from the bottle. 'Dad's a proud man. He doesn't want pity, and he hates me fussing. But you can understand why I wanted to stay close at hand, in case he…needs me.'

'Of course…' she said, yet another of Della's rock-solid assumptions where this man was concerned disintegrating. 'Is he badly affected?'

He looked away, focused on the setting sun, as if he no longer wanted to talk about it. 'He's still managing his activities of daily living, but he struggles with the stairs. I've moved his bed to the ground floor, but ideally, I'd like him to sell up and move into an adapted bungalow.'

Della stayed silent, understanding both sides of the argument. Bill would fiercely cling to his independence, and as an only child, Harvey just wanted peace of mind that his father was safe.

'Anyway…' he said, dragging out the word to herald a change of subject. 'Back to my earlier question, before we were interrupted by our emergency. No dates in three and half years? How's that working out for you?'

Della sighed. Jerk Harvey was back. Only she could no longer hate him for beating her to her dream job, and she still needed to apologise for using him for sex. At this rate, with her justifications dissolving before her eyes, she risked becoming his…*friend*. No, the attraction would always get in the way of that. But now that she had to let go of her bitterness over losing the position to Harvey, she realised how she'd used it as a shield from thinking about that incredible night when she'd learned the stories about Harvey were true. He *was* good at everything.

'No need to sound so astounded,' she said haughtily. 'It's not fatal. I'm not ready for another relationship yet.' The last thing she wanted to discuss with Harvey was the breakdown of her marriage, the mistake she'd made in trusting Ethan, the humiliation of her divorce, when all she wanted was to be like her brother: happily married and starting a family.

'Who said anything about relationships?' Harvey asked, his stare holding hers the way it had in the ED doctors' office before they attended to the emergency, as if he could see straight through her to all her failings and weaknesses. 'I'm talking about sex.'

He took another swallow of beer and licked his lips the way Della wanted to. She swallowed, her throat bone-dry with lust. Harvey was the last man on Earth she wanted to discuss her sad lack of a sex life with.

His stare narrowed, his scrutiny making her flustered. 'So, are you saying that *your* last time was *our* last time?' he asked, incredulous.

'What if it was?' Della snapped, all the empathy she'd felt for him a moment ago evaporating. 'You can't make a competition out of my personal life, Harvey.'

Because he'd win that argument, too. With that single exception, when she'd succumbed to Harvey Ward's charms, she'd lived like a nun since her divorce. It wasn't healthy, but Della had always needed an emotional connection to even think about being intimate with someone. That didn't make her a prude, just a woman.

'But you can make a joke out of *my* personal life?' he asked, his expression as calm as the sea before them. 'I like sex. Don't you?'

She felt his observation all over her body. Of course she liked sex. Why was that question so arousing and tempting, as if it was an offer?

'Don't goad me,' she snapped, 'just because we're different. I'm not like you.'

She looked away, hot and bothered. Why did she always allow him to get to her like this? Why couldn't she simply ignore him the way she'd tried to over the years? Because when it came to Brody's best friend, it had always been easier to dismiss and avoid him than to admit his relationship self-sufficiency, his easy-breezy attitude to dating, his cynicism about love only highlighted their differences and made Della feel somehow inadequate, reigniting those fears that she was being left behind in her family. She'd always wanted a loving, committed relationship and a family of her own, whereas Harvey didn't even believe in love.

But there was no chance of ignoring him now that they had to spend the best part of the next two weeks working together. No wonder she was feeling volatile.

'In what way are we different?' he asked, appearing genuinely curious. 'I think we have a surprising amount in common, considering we're always arguing.'

Della dragged in a deep breath. She wanted to point out that *he* was responsible for their bickering, but she held back. They were finally going to have a meaningful conversation, after all the years of avoiding it with polite smiles and impersonal comments and, on Della's part, cowardice and self-preservation.

'Oh, come on, Harvey,' she said warily, 'we're total opposites, especially when it comes to relationships. And don't pretend that we could ever get along. You've never even liked me.'

Harvey took another lazy swallow of beer, his eyes on hers. 'I like you just fine, Della.'

The husky drawl of his voice turned her limbs molten with desire. Was that true? Did he like her? Admitting that he might be telling the truth, that Harvey did have another, deeper side, sat like a rock in her stomach, reminding her how she *had* used him for sex that night and he'd probably not only known it but also felt hurt.

'If you like me so much,' she said, on the attack, jittery with nerves from his admission, 'why take the moral high ground when it comes to our differences? To relationships? It's as if you see the kind of commitment most people want, the kind *I* want, as some sort of threat. As if you're too smart to fall in love like the rest of us, or you think love is a joke.'

'I don't think that at all,' he said, looking mildly uncomfortable for the first time. 'We've just always wanted different things. But you've done your fair share of judging, Della, right from the moment we met.'

'Well, you insulted me,' she said, aware she was overreacting and dragging up ancient history. 'We'd just been introduced, and you felt comfortable enough to point out my relationship at the time was doomed. In fact, you've objected to every one of my past boyfriends for some reason or another,' she continued. 'You didn't even like Ethan, as if *you,* the great relationship expert, Harvey Ward, were somehow privy to inside knowledge that our marriage wouldn't last.' She hated that he'd been right, *again*. That unlike Della, he'd shown good judgement when it came to her ex. No wonder she wasn't ready to trust her intuition and risk another relationship just yet. Perhaps she should take a leaf out of Harvey's book and enjoy a casual sexual fling.

'And you've always objected to *me*,' he said, eyes glittering. 'As if I wasn't a good enough friend for Brody or good enough to be associated with your family, just because I prefer to be single.'

Della sat back in outrage. 'See, this always happens. We're fooling ourselves if we expect to make it through two weeks of working together. We're too different, too competitive to ever get along.' She glugged a mouthful of beer, looking away from him in disgust. The Wiltons were an ambitious bunch, and Harvey fit right in. Della had struggled growing up in golden boy Brody's exalted footsteps, and then, just when she'd started to make her own mark by getting into medical school, he'd brought home driven, talented Harvey.

'We can do it if we have to,' he said calmly, where Della was braced for another battle. 'We didn't argue that night in bed. Or have you forgotten?'

Despite her temper, Della's body incinerated. She scowled at him. 'How could I forget when over the years I've heard so many wild stories of your sex life from Brody?' She leaned forward, needing to win this argument. 'The threesomes. The heartbroken women past their expiration dates. Your rotating bedroom door and your untouchable heart.'

Harvey's lip curled, his stare narrowing as he watched her with curiosity. 'It was *one* threesome, and that was years ago.' His dark gaze rested on her lips. 'But you sound jealous, Della. We can rectify that.' He spread his arms wide and relaxed back in the chair in a *come and get me* gesture.

Every cell in her body perked up, his offer beyond tempting. How would she fight this physical compulsion for two whole weeks? Not even them bickering seemed to douse the flames. 'Oh please...' Della scoffed, her body temperature high with irritation and fierce desire. 'I am *so* done with men.'

Of course, he was right; they were good together. Great, in fact. A big part of her wanted another go at Harvey if for no other reason than to wipe that smug look off his face.

'Hey,' Harvey said, holding up a hand to ward off her unfair comparison, 'don't go bringing your ex into this again.' He took another swig of beer, cool, calm and collected.

Della dragged in a ragged breath. She was being over-emotional. She didn't care one jot if Harvey slept with every other woman on the planet *but* her. Time to change the subject.

'Why didn't you like Ethan,' she asked, a lump

in her throat, 'just out of interest?' She shouldn't care; her marriage and divorce were *her* business. But the part of her that had always compared herself to golden boy Brody and then later to carefree Harvey was scared to completely trust her own judgement. Had she missed some sign that others had seen? Ethan had wooed her with a whirlwind romance, proposed after a couple of years and then slowly changed once they were married. And Della hadn't seen the divorce coming.

'Let's not go there.' Harvey instantly sobered, glancing away. 'It's in the past, and it's nothing to do with me.' He clenched his jaw as if he had no intention of answering her question.

'Come on, I want to know,' Della pushed, her curiosity so wild, her heart rate went through the roof. It must be bad if he was refusing to say. Hot shame washed through her. It was bad enough that she'd failed at something Brody had nailed—a successful marriage and a family. Even worse that Harvey, of all people, had witnessed Della's defeat and now seemed to have some kind of insider knowledge.

'Leave it, Della.' Harvey frowned as he made eye contact, warning in his stare. 'You won't like what I have to say. We'll end up arguing again.'

'Tell me anyway,' she demanded, embarrassment a head-to-toe itchy rash. 'I insist.' Had there been some glaringly obvious flaw in her and Ethan's relationship? Had outsiders deduced what Della herself hadn't seen coming? Had Harvey correctly predicted that her marriage had been doomed?

With a sigh, Harvey reluctantly surrendered. 'I've known you since you were eighteen, Della. You wear your big heart on your sleeve. Fall in love and dive in, as if… I don't know. As if you somehow have something to prove. As if you're in competition with every other couple out there.'

Della gasped, mortified. 'I've also grown up since you first met me, Harvey.' Although she couldn't help but compare herself to her brother. She shrank inside, feeling sick. How dare untouchable Harvey, her nemesis, know her so well. How dare he see her need to be loved and to be accepted as she was so effortlessly when he didn't know the first thing about the emotion. Could he also see her deepest fear, that by pushing for a family, she'd pushed Ethan away?

'Trust me,' she continued with a scoff, bluffing for all she was worth, 'I have no interest in exposing my heart or diving into another relationship until I'm certain the lucky guy wants exactly what *I* want.'

She'd learned her mistake with Ethan. At the end, he'd accused her of being *baby obsessed*, even though when they'd met, he'd said he too wanted a family. But next time she was ready for a relationship, it would be with someone who, like her, wanted it all: commitment, marriage, a family. Yet how could she ever be certain they were being truthful when Ethan had managed to dupe her?

'Good…' Harvey shrugged, his expression full of regret as if he hated what he was about to say. 'Because sometimes…little things he said… I just got the impression that Ethan was… I don't know…holding something back.'

Della froze, wishing she hadn't asked but some sick twisted part of her willing him to continue.

'When you got engaged,' he said, his stare searching hers, 'I genuinely hoped for your sake that I was wrong. That it would work out. That you'd be happy.'

Her eyes stung. She absolutely must not cry in front of Harvey. *Never ever.* Because he was right. When they'd met and fallen in love, Ethan had claimed he'd wanted the same things. But once they'd married, once they'd fallen into a routine of work and sharing a home, he'd started putting off their conversations about starting a family, made her feel as if the dream was suddenly one-sided. He'd used her desire to have it all to make her feel that *his* job was more important. Shamefully, she'd followed him to Sydney so he could pursue *his* career, reasoning that someone had to compromise. But even after his big promotion, he'd continued to put off talk of kids. Della had given the marriage her all, and delayed becoming a mother while Ethan established himself in an orthopaedic consultant role, but it hadn't been enough. He'd come home one day and said he wasn't ready to be a father and left. And Della had been blindsided. But *Harvey*, a man who knew nothing about relationships, had somehow predicted it.

Returning to the present, Della blinked, shivered, chilled to the bone. Harvey's concerned face came back into focus, something like pity in his stare. Her stomach turned with sickening humiliation.

'Well, bravo, Harvey—you were right, again,' she said, shame and failure a fire in her blood. 'You, who don't even believe in love, saw my marriage the way it truly was. But then, you'd know all about holding back, wouldn't you? You've never had a relationship. Do you even possess a heart, Harvey? Or are all those messy human emotions for the rest of us poor misguided fools?'

How could she have been so stupid as to consider sleeping with him again? They were polar opposites, too competitive and threatened by each other to ever see eye to eye. They couldn't even have one simple conversation.

'I don't think that,' he said, reaching for her arm.

But the damage was done. Della snatched it out of his reach. Rising to her feet, she shoved the seat back so hard, it toppled to the sand. 'I'll see you tomorrow,' she said, for once her voice staying impressively calm. 'Can I suggest that, for the sake of harmony, to make the next two weeks even remotely bearable, that we restrict our conversations to work, after all.' Without waiting for an answer, she stomped off.

CHAPTER FOUR

DELLA ENTERED HER staff bungalow on the hospital grounds and slammed the door. The reverberations jolted through Harvey from his position across the street. He'd followed her, of course. He'd never have been able to sleep if he hadn't made certain she'd arrived home safely.

He dragged in a shuddering breath, guilt making him cringe. He should never have allowed himself to be lured into a personal conversation. They couldn't be trusted not to bicker, insult and upset each other. Then she'd forced him to talk about her ex, demanding he be honest, before throwing his reluctant observations back in his face.

Why could they never have a nice, normal chat? Maybe because the attraction was always there, bubbling away beneath the surface. Harvey *hadn't* liked any of her boyfriends. She was right. None of them were good enough for her, not even Ethan. She was funny and smart and would do anything for anyone, and after today,

Harvey had gained a massive amount of respect for her as a surgeon.

Harvey crossed the road, regret a weight on his shoulders. What the hell did he know about committed relationships anyway? He'd been alone by choice for twenty years, after Alice had died in a car accident. He'd assumed he'd get over her death in time and want another relationship, but as the years had passed, he'd become increasingly convinced that he should have known better than to pin his happiness on another person. After all, if his own mother hadn't loved him enough to stick around, what hope did he have of finding someone with whom he could share his life?

Harvey tapped on the door to Della's bungalow, his gut twisting. The last thing he wanted to do was hurt Della. Why would she care what *he* had to say? But maybe she saw her divorce as some sort of failing, even though it was her ex who chose to leave the marriage.

The door flew open, as if she'd been standing and fuming on the other side.

'You left your sunnies at the bar,' he said, wearing an apologetic expression as he held out the sunglasses.

'Thanks.' She took them, dropping them onto the table just inside the door. When she looked at him again, her stare brimmed with hurt that he'd inadvertently put there because, ever since that night three years ago, he couldn't seem to manage this attraction.

'I'm sorry, Della,' he said, contrite. 'I didn't mean to hurt you. My comments were...thoughtless. I don't think you're a fool for falling in love. The opposite, in fact.' He stared into her blue eyes, forcing himself to open up in order to repair the damage. 'It's not that I don't believe in love. It's more that making yourself vulnerable with another person is a brave gamble. But then, I'm hardly an expert. As you pointed out, what do *I* know about relationships?'

She eyed him hesitantly, still wearing a frown.

'You shouldn't listen to me,' he went on. 'I just wouldn't want you to be hurt again, that's all. If I'm honest, I didn't like your boyfriends because none of them were good enough for you.'

He shut his mouth, suddenly exhausted. He'd already given away how protective he felt of her, when he had no right. Her love life was none of his business, and *he* wasn't the man of anyone's dreams. At least she was brave enough to put herself out there, whereas he simply avoided the risk of letting someone close, of giving them the power to cause pain. When it came to matters of the heart, *she* was the experienced one.

Della sighed, her body relaxing. 'I *did* push for your honest opinion,' she said, shaking her head with regret. 'And I threw my fair share of insults your way. Maybe I just hate that you're always right. That, like Brody, you're better than me at *everything*.' Her lips twitched with amusement, telling him he was forgiven.

Harvey's pulse pounded with relief, but his stare raked hers. Did she compare herself unfavourably to Brody? Harvey was an only child, so he had no reference when it came to sibling rivalry.

'Not everything,' he said, a cautious smile forming. 'Definitely not relationships.' Harvey's parents had split when he was kid, so as far as he was concerned, relationship breakdowns were inevitable. Maybe it was time to tell Della about Alice, about his mother, about why the cynical twenty-three-year-old she'd met had been so down on commitment and still was, if pushed.

'Only because you've never had one,' she said, rolling her eyes. 'If you had, I'm sure that, like Brody, you'd have made it work. You'd probably be living *my* life by now—successful career, happily married, a houseful of adorable children.'

Harvey hid a wince, wishing he could say something to help reassure Della that she still had time to achieve her dreams, but he'd already overstepped the mark once tonight. He hated that she wanted what Brody had, but had been let down by her ex. Maybe once, a long time ago, Harvey might have harboured that same dream, back when he'd thought he was in control of his life and his heart. But growing up abandoned by his mother, the only woman who should have loved him unconditionally, had taught him that feelings, entrusting your happiness to another person, was a big risk. And he'd re-learned that same lesson the hard way when Alice had died.

'Well, if it's any consolation,' he said, steering the conversation back to the relative safety of work, 'having seen you in action in the OR today, I'd say you can hold your own as a surgeon with both me and Brody.' Respect for her bloomed anew. She was a good doctor and a talented surgeon, damn sexy qualities. But then, everything about Della was sexy and always had been. Probably why he goaded her. Nothing worse than forbidden fruit to increase ardour. And apart from that one lapse, when he'd kissed her back, one thing leading to another, Harvey was smart enough to stay well away. They wanted different things in life. Della wanted that marriage, husband, a houseful of kids dream, and Harvey liked being in control of his life and his emotions. So why was he struggling to walk away now?

'Careful, Harvey.' She smiled, eyed in him in that way that heated his blood, but also told him she could laugh at herself and at him. 'That sounds suspiciously like another compliment.'

He dragged in a shaky breath. 'Good. It is. Will you be okay?' He hesitated on the doorstep, needing to know that their stupid fight hadn't caused lasting damage to Della's self-esteem. He should leave. Let her get some sleep before their seminars in the morning. But he cared about her and genuinely wanted to see her happy.

'Of course.' She blinked, watched him with curiosity as if seeing him for the first time. 'I'm a strong, independent and resilient woman. It will take more than one little divorce to keep me down.'

'I know you are,' he said, seeing through her bravado. Those old protective urges resurfaced. The Harvey that had first met this woman had known all about the pain of heartbreak. It had been hard to stand on the sidelines and watch big-hearted Della go through break-up after break-up and finally her divorce. Not that looking out for her, back then or now, was his place.

'Okay… I'll…um…let you get some rest.' He took a half step back, his feet dragging. Being trapped with her in Fiji had forced him to admit how badly he still wanted her, how the grip he thought he had on his attraction was weakened because he couldn't avoid temptation and walk away the way he had three years ago, the way he did every time he'd seen her since. Nor could he shake the knowledge that she hadn't had sex with another man since him, that she still wasn't ready for a relationship. And if he needed one more sign that this trip had been sent to test him and his belief that Della was out of his system, she was looking at him in *that* way again.

'Thanks…' she said, touching his arm. 'For the sunglasses *and* the compliment. It means a lot coming from you.'

Her touch burned his skin, her words an acknowledgement that they might be different, but when it came to work, they respected each other.

'You're welcome.' His voice was scratchy. His feet didn't seem to want to move.

'You know,' she said, blinking up at him, 'I'm sorry, too.' Her breathing came faster. 'I *did* use you for sex that night. You were right about that, as well.' She blushed and Harvey shrugged it off, his pulse roaring because she was still touching his arm.

'That's okay. Truth is, I was happy to be used.' What kind of idiot would turn down sex with someone as gorgeous as Della, even if he had been her rebound? He'd never forgotten that night, probably because Della Wilton, like the rest of her loving, boisterous family, was a massive part of his life. But they really shouldn't discuss sex any more tonight or he'd never make it off this doorstep.

'I wanted to feel attractive again after, you know, being rejected,' she said, looking down and then meeting his stare. 'But it's not okay that I hurt you in the process.'

Harvey understood rejection, but were they declaring a truce? 'You're beautiful, Della. And I'm a grown man. I wanted you too much to care about your motivations.' Adrenaline rushed through his system. It felt good to admit that after all these years of pretending he didn't find her incredibly attractive. But this was dangerous territory.

Her eyes widened. Time slowed as they stared. What was it about this place that completely altered the nature of their relationship? It was as if for the first time ever they were being honest. Finally, Harvey tilted his head in resignation and stepped back. If he didn't leave now, he was going to do something stupid. And this time, there'd be no walking away, no pretending it hadn't happened, at least not until they left Fiji.

'Wait,' she said, reaching for the hem of his shirt and tugging. 'Don't go.'

He crossed the threshold. She closed the door, pulled him closer.

'Della…is this a good idea?' His hands found her waist, neither drawing her close nor holding her distant. Their bodies were inches apart. The heat of her, the subtle scent of her perfume, called to that part of him he'd always needed to lock down in her presence.

'It's just sex, Harvey,' she argued with a shrug, tossing back his earlier words. 'Best to get it out of the way so we can move on and work together, don't you think?'

Think…? All of his blood had left his brain. Thinking was impossible. But his instincts were still firing. 'I want you, but I don't want to hurt you again or give you the wrong idea about us. You know me.' They were too different for more than sex. Under all her bluff and bluster, Della was a funny, caring and wildly passionate woman any guy looking to settle down would be lucky to have. But Harvey wasn't that guy, and they both knew it.

'Come on, Harvey.' She blinked up at him, her stare dark with desire and unspoken challenge. 'I'm an intelligent woman. I'd never be stupid enough to expect anything but sex from a man like *you*.'

Reassurance dressed as an insult, but she was right. She knew him the way he knew her. He wasn't relationship material, and Della wanted it all. Of course, she didn't know everything about his past—some ugliness was too uncomfortable to share—but she knew enough to have realistic expectations.

'Are you worried that I'm using you for sex again?' she asked, a playful glint in her blue eyes. 'Because if it helps, I totally am.'

Harvey fought his instincts. He should have felt relieved that they were on the same page. That just like last time, Della wasn't looking for anything serious. But somewhere deep down, her words—*a man like you...using you for sex again*—also stung. Despite what she believed, Harvey *did* possess a heart. He'd just trained it to have very low expectations.

'I'm not worried,' he lied, clinging to reason as she inched closer, her breasts grazing his chest. He gripped her face, tilted that lovely mouth up to within a whisper of his. 'I just want you to be sure. Eyes wide open like last time.'

'I want you.' Della held his stare as she surged up on tiptoe and sought his mouth with hers. She gripped his neck and pulled him down, closing the distance. Della knew what she wanted, and she was right—this was the best way to break the tension so they could get through two weeks of forced proximity.

Too late to overthink it, Harvey crushed her close. The first touch of their kiss flooded his strung-out body with energising endorphins. Their lips parted. Tongues met, surged, tasted.

A sense of déjà vu struck, as if he recalled every detail of the last time they kissed. As if they aligned perfectly.

'Harvey...' Della moaned as he slid his lips down the side of her neck.

His name on her lips shifted something primal and urgent inside him, so he pressed her body closer. Selfishly, on some level, Harvey needed to know that Della wanted him for no other reason than this fierce, immoveable attraction. This time, there was no ghost of another man to chase off. This was about *them*.

'Why is it that we get on so much better without words,' she panted, sliding her hands inside his T-shirt, her palms branding his skin.

'I have no idea.' Harvey backed her up, pressing her against the wall to increase the contact between their bodies. Maybe it was because words were open to misinterpretation, whereas physically, they just clicked. Harvey ground his hips against hers, urgency to be inside her pounding through his veins. Della angled her head, exposing her neck to his kisses. Then she shoved up his shirt, yanking it over his head and tossing it before removing her own.

He looked down to where her breasts were encased in sexy black lace. 'I swear you get sexier each time I see you.' And he was only human. Della was too sexy to ignore when she was on the other side of the room shooting him disapproving looks. Like this, seductive, needy in his arms, saying all the right things, he'd had no hope of resisting.

Kissing her again, he hoisted her from the floor so she wrapped her legs around his waist, her fingers demanding in his hair. She moaned as he cupped one breast through her bra, kissing his jaw, his neck, the notch between his collarbones while her hips undulated against his. Harvey's eyes rolled closed, the friction between their writhing bodies almost unbearable.

'Hold tight,' he said, slinging his arms under her butt and striding to the bedroom. He placed her on her feet, and she unclasped and removed her bra.

'Hurry,' she said, tugging at the waistband of his shorts. 'It's been three years.'

'Whose fault is that?' Harvey smiled as he popped the button on her sexy denim cut-off shorts, then scooped her back into his arms. Their naked chests pressed together, and he walked them back towards the bed. 'Besides, that's all the more reason not to rush.'

Ducking his head, he captured first one of her nipples in his mouth and then the other.

'See,' she gasped, her head falling back, 'you always need to be right, even now.'

'And you always need to have the last word.'

He grinned, laying her down on the bed. He unzipped her shorts and slid them and her underwear down her shapely legs.

For a second he simply stared, swaying on his feet. She was glowing, beautiful, her stare heavy with desire. A knot formed under his ribs. This might be just sex, but Della was precious, almost family, as much a part of the furniture in his life as the rest of the Wiltons. He couldn't afford to mess this up just because he wanted her and the feeling was mutual.

'Don't overthink it, Harvey,' she said, holding out her hand for his. 'Just come here.'

Before he got too carried away by temptation, Harvey removed his wallet from his pocket, took out a condom and placed it on the bed. Then he kicked off his shoes and took her hand, lying down at her side.

'Kiss me,' she demanded, wrapping her arms around his shoulders and hooking one leg over his hip so his doubts were silenced.

He cupped her backside and pushed his tongue against hers, laughing when she rolled him onto his back and sat astride him.

'So it's like that, is it?' he asked, toying with her nipples as she leaned over him to kiss him once more. He didn't mind her being on top or making demands or using him for sex. He'd grown accustomed over the years to the power

play in his every interaction with Della, and he liked her playful side. She groaned as his hands skimmed her waist, her hips, guiding them to rock against his hard length.

'Stop teasing me,' she ordered, kissing him with renewed desperation.

When he rolled them again, tore his mouth from hers and trailed kisses down her neck, chest and stomach, she sighed in surrender. Going lower, he spread her thighs and covered her with his mouth. She cried out, her fingers spearing his hair. He wanted to take his time, to savour her, to unleash more of that wildly passionate Della that had blown him away three years ago. Her moans intensified. He pushed his fingers inside her and groaned as she tensed, gasped, climaxed, crying out his name once more. Triumph expanded his chest. If she'd waited three years, he wanted to-night to be memorable. She was right; this was their best form of communication. They didn't need feelings or hurtful words or one-upman-ship. Just touch and honest desire.

'You are so sexy,' he said, shoving off his shorts and briefs. He rolled on the condom and kissed his way back up her satiated body.

'Don't be smug,' she whispered, smiling and breathless, drawing his mouth back to hers as she wrapped her hand around his erection.

'I'm afraid you can't stop me.' He grinned,

gripped her thigh and drew it over his hip so he sank between her legs. 'Three years *is* a long time. Did you think about us?' He had.

'I might have done, on occasion,' she admitted begrudgingly, her pupils dilating as she snagged her lip with her teeth. 'But you don't need your ego stroking.'

Too late. With his heart thudding triumphantly because he hadn't been alone in reliving that night, Harvey laughed and swooped in for another kiss. Even after her orgasm, when admitting that they were hot together—that, like him, she'd struggled to forget—Della needed to come out on top. But with them naked and pleasuring each other rather than fighting, there was no point hiding how good they were together physically.

'Go slow,' she whispered, spreading her legs, inviting him into her body with a teasing tilt of her hips.

He pushed inside her, their stares locked. 'I thought about us, too,' he admitted, fighting his instincts to move.

Her eyes widened, a small gasp leaving her throat.

'Every time I saw you, I wanted you again, even while we fought and bickered and tried to pretend it hadn't happened.' He moved inside her body, his heart banging against hers.

'I wanted you, too,' she gasped as he thrust faster. Della tunnelled her fingers into his hair and drew his lips to hers, pushed her tongue into his mouth so he groaned. They'd never stood a chance of ignoring this attraction, this connection. They were too good together. Their sparks were exceptional. Fighting it was almost a crime against sex.

As he found the perfect rhythm, Harvey fought his own need. He wanted her with him, a tied race. He wanted her as consumed as him, so that they might move on, but they'd never forget.

'Harvey,' Della gasped, and he kissed her, cupped her beautiful breasts, thumbed her nipples erect and watched as desire darkened her blue eyes to navy.

'Come with me,' he said, picking up the pace so Della cried out and crossed her ankles in the small of his back, her fingernails digging into his arms. Harvey bent one knee for purchase, driving harder and faster. As fire raced down his spine, Harvey sent her tumbling over the edge once more, finally following her with a harsh groan, his body racked with spasms. He buried his face in the crook of her neck, sucked in the scent of her skin and wrung every drop of pleasure from their bodies.

Finally he released Della to collapse, satiated, at her side. They stared at the ceiling, both panting.

'Why did I wait so long?' Della asked, a satisfied smile stretching her lips.

'Beats me...' Harvey grinned. He'd been absolutely right about their unfinished business. But as the oxygen returned to his brain, awareness returned. Reason. Sense. Yes, their chemistry was still explosive, but it was also still something to be very wary of. Because neither of them had changed in the past three years. They still wanted different things when it came to relationships.

As he scooped a breathless Della into his arms, Harvey gritted his teeth, prepared for a fierce internal battle of desire for her, for *this*, versus self-preservation. Two weeks didn't feel like a long time, but if they kept being intimate, it was long enough to form a habit. When it came to relationships, he'd spent years fighting that kind of trap, keeping people out.

Surely he could survive thirteen more days until he could put some distance between himself and the temptation of Della?

CHAPTER FIVE

THE NEXT MORNING in the seminar room, Della tried to focus on Harvey's talk on sports-related trauma, but her mind kept wandering. Had last night really happened? How had they gone from arguing in Savu's to sleeping together again? Oh, she'd instigated it by asking him to stay. The minute he'd stood on the doorstep and apologised, the minute he'd opened up, let her in, hinting at his beliefs on love, the minute he'd alluded to the fact that, despite appearances, he'd always had a thing for her, all the anger and humiliation inside her had drained away.

How could she stay angry with Harvey, when she'd always had a thing for him too? When she'd seen another side to him? And how could the sex between them have been better than the last time? They'd had sex three times—the second time in the shower and again in bed before finally collapsing into a state of replete exhaustion. She'd awoken at dawn to the unfamiliar heat and sounds of a tropical island and nudged

Harvey awake. He'd untangled his limbs from hers, kissed her, dressed and rushed back to his own bungalow, giving Della a brief reprieve to come to terms with the fact that Harvey seemed to be hotter than ever before.

How was that even possible, let alone fair? And what did it mean for her attempts to resist him? Dragging her gaze from the man in question, Della glanced around the room. A small audience, predominantly doctors and physiotherapists from the hospital with a handful of local GPs, listened to Harvey talk. Della zoned back into what he was saying, their eyes briefly meeting, before he looked back down at his notes.

Shivers of both delight and dread danced down her spine. What was he thinking? Did he want this physical fling to continue for the duration of their time in Fiji, or was he done? He was giving little away, although he could hardly look at her the way he had last night in front of an audience. Della herself was horribly confused. On the one hand, having incredible sex with Harvey was better than two weeks of arguing. They were trapped there, after all. But was it wise? She'd never known Harvey to see a woman more than a few times. Would he even be up for a holiday fling? Or should they agree to put the sex behind them again and simply focus on working together? Her stomach sank at the thought. But just because she still wanted him, just because she'd witnessed a deeper side to Harvey she hadn't known existed, she'd do well to remember that when it came to relationships, they were total opposites. She sighed; she was talking herself around in circles.

The audience broke into a round of applause, and Della joined in. Harvey's talk had obviously concluded, although she'd missed most of it with her lusty daydreams.

'Thank you, Dr Ward,' Dr Tora said. 'A very informative update. We'll take a fifteen-minute break. Refreshments are available out on the veranda.'

While Harvey was approached by an audience member with a question, Della stepped outside and helped herself to a glass of iced water. There was no point trying to eat. Her stomach was too full of butterflies, her head too full of the dilemma. In theory, a little holiday sex hurt no one, especially when she and Harvey understood each other so well. At this moment, Della wasn't ready for more than sex, and even when that changed, she'd never consider Harvey. He didn't do relationships. So where was the harm in a brief sexual fling? But could she spend all this time with him, explore a sexual relationship that was obviously heading nowhere, and keep emotional boundaries in place?

'Thanks for the wake-up call,' a deep voice said over her shoulder, jolting her out of her thoughts.

Della hid a delicious shudder of anticipation, turning to offer Harvey a tight, professional smile as if they were no more than colleagues. 'You're welcome. The sunrise woke me.' Finding Harvey's big, manly body sprawled in her bed, taking up more than his fair share of space, she'd watched him sleep for a few indulgent seconds, carefully sniffing the scent of his shampoo and memorising the small scar on his shoulder. Even asleep, he was outrageously handsome.

'So…how are you feeling today?' he asked in a low voice, taking a sip of what smelled like strong black coffee, his favourite. 'Any regrets? I know I'm not your favourite person.' His voice was light as he watched her intently over the rim of his cup, his playful reminder well-timed. They'd been adversaries for so long. Could they truly be lovers, even temporarily?

'Hmm…' Della kept her expression serious and pretended to think about it. 'I guess I can live with what happened, given *I* was the one to instigate it.' She didn't want him thinking last night was his idea. 'How about you?' she asked, with a twitch of a smile. 'Have you booked the first flight out of here and deleted me from your contacts yet?'

Just because he'd admitted he'd thought all of her boyfriends including her ex-husband unworthy didn't mean their very different views on commitment and love had changed. What had he called it? A *brave gamble*? But why?

Harvey shrugged, his stare flirtatious. 'Not quite yet.'

Della fought a smile and looked down. There was a perfectly professional distance between his body and hers. To the outsider, they might be having a medicine-related conversation. Instead, her body was aflame. How could zero physical contact generate so many sparks?

'When you think about it,' she said, emboldened but her heart galloping with nerves, 'holiday flings are pretty harmless.' A safe, casual sex fling might do her a world of good. She searched his stare for any sign that he was done, although this was Harvey—short-lived flings were his forte. But if he was waiting for her to beg, he'd be waiting a long time.

'Hmm… They do have considerable benefits.' Harvey nodded, his expression thoughtful. 'A nice, neat end date when you fly home to the real world.'

Holding her nerve, she waited. She refused to crack until he cracked first. But surely they were on the same page? Surely them sleeping together benefited them working together harmoniously?

Flushed from her shameful justifications, Della held her breath as Harvey inched closer and dipped his head. 'As long as both parties use the other for the same thing, of course.'

Heartened, she caught a flicker of excitement in his eyes. Mentally, she raised a victory fist. She was willing to be used for sex, as long as she could use him in return.

'Of course. And this Fiji. Different rules apply,' she added, looking for his agreement. 'Once we leave this island, usual business resumes.'

'I agree,' he said, a small frown tugging at his mouth. 'Because we *will* see each other again.'

Della nodded, the warning clear. It was the same debate she'd been ruminating on all morning. Yes, their affair would end, but they couldn't ghost each other. Harvey would still be Brody's best friend, and Della would still see him at Wilton family functions.

'But by then,' she went on, reassuring herself as much as Harvey, 'we will have each moved on. Melbourne has a very active singles scene, I believe.' Harvey would find ample casual distractions once he returned to Australia. As they said, a leopard never changed its spots.

Harvey's stare intensified with that flicker of challenge she was used to. 'And maybe you'll find everything you want in Auckland—that devoted husband, a houseful of adorable children. You already have the successful career part.'

See, they knew each other so well. Uninvited, his words from the night before rushed Della's mind... *It's not that I don't believe in love...* Last night, she'd been too upset with him to give the statement much thought. But now it niggled at her. Was this another of Harvey's hidden depths? Was there some reason he'd sworn off relationships beyond his general cynicism following his parents' divorce?

'So, where does that leave us, I wonder?' she asked, dismissing the idea, because his motivations for staying single changed nothing. Harvey would likely never cancel his membership to the singles club, and Della still wanted it all with the right man. She wasn't stupid. There was no way she and Harvey, of all men, could be anything serious. She'd already made one big mistake with Ethan. Next time she risked her heart, she'd make sure the man was all in.

'I guess the door is still open to possibility,' he said cryptically, his stare sparking with heat, the expression doing silly things to Della's pulse. How could she still want him after last night? She'd lost count of how many orgasms she'd had, but it would be so easy to become addicted to sex that good.

'Speaking of possibility,' he said, stepping

back so they were once more that respectable distance apart, 'I wondered if you'd like to explore one of the smaller islands with me later, as we have the afternoon off? We could rent a kayak and some snorkel gear. There's no point wasting the fantastic downtime opportunities.'

'That sounds good,' she said, visualising other opportunities—them alone and naked. 'As long as it's not Mallau Island,' she added with a mock grimace. 'I spent my ill-fated honeymoon there.' She offered him a wry smile, shoving all thoughts of Ethan from her mind. She'd moved on, her biggest regret that she hadn't seen through him sooner and saved herself both time and heartache.

But Harvey sobered, a small frown lodging between his brows. 'I wouldn't want to bring up any painful reminders for you. Why don't *you* choose our destination. A clean slate.'

'I will,' Della said breezily, hoping to reassure him, while enjoying that he was…protective. 'Don't look so worried. Mallau isn't the only stunning island in the archipelago.' There were over three hundred.

'In that case,' Harvey said, leaning in a little closer and dropping his voice, 'I'll do my best to keep your mind very much in the present and help you make some new memories.' The innocently phrased promise dripped with suggestion, filling Della with the thrilling fizz of anticipation.

'No, *I'll* help *you* make some,' she breathed, already looking forward to exploring Fiji with Harvey. Despite a worrying start, her working holiday had taken a very unexpected but pleasurable turn. Maybe two weeks trapped with Harvey in paradise wouldn't be so bad after all.

Just then, Dr Tora appeared from the seminar room, his face tense with concern. 'Excuse me, everyone,' he called. 'There's been a vehicle collision off the King's Road north of here. A minibus full of backpackers left the road and ploughed downhill into the dense bush. There are multiple casualties expected in the emergency department shortly. Can everyone who's available please head there to help where they can?'

As he spoke, multiple pagers sounded around them, urgent calls to their Fijian colleagues coming thick and fast.

Della and Harvey glanced at each other and abandoned their drinks. Their afternoon off, their downtime together—exploring, snorkelling, falling into bed—would have to wait. Duty called. They took off running, making it to the ED a few minutes later, in time to intercept the first wave of casualties.

'We have a twenty-three-year-old male with

a penetrating abdominal wound,' the paramedic handing over a patient said as he wheeled the stretcher into a vacant resuscitation bay.

'He was flung from the window and impaled on a broken tree branch,' the paramedic continued. 'He has IV access, and I've given him morphine and IV fluids. Blood pressure is on the low side, but he's been conscious throughout.'

The casualty groaned in pain. Della sprang into action, listening to the young man's chest and abdominal sounds as nursing staff connected him to heart monitors and oxygen and began cutting away his clothing. A junior ED doctor drew blood from the man's arm to cross-match for a blood transfusion.

Harvey removed the dressing and exposed the wound in the patient's abdomen. A five-centimetre-diameter tree branch protruded from the wound just under his ribs on the right.

Della met Harvey's stare, seeing her concerns mirrored there. The risk of internal haemorrhage with injuries of this nature was high. This patient would need an urgent laparotomy to assess the internal damage and remove the branch. But if he was bleeding internally, first he must be stabilised.

'Let's get four units of blood cross-matched,' Harvey called to the junior ED doctor. 'Any sign of pneumothorax?' he asked Della, reaching for his own stethoscope.

'No,' she said, drawing up some more analgesia, 'but it will be a miracle if this has avoided his liver.'

Harvey nodded, his expression grim. They needed to operate on the man as soon as possible.

'I need an infusion of intravenous antibiotics, please,' Della said to Seema, the ED nurse, keeping one eye on the blood pressure monitor. Before her eyes, the pressure dropped. Her stare darted to Harvey, a different kind of adrenaline flooding her system. As if making a joint decision, Harvey nodded to Della and unlocked the wheels of the stretcher.

'Send the blood round to theatre,' he said, his voice calm but full of authority. 'Dr Wilton and I are taking him straight to surgery.'

It was the same call Della would have made. There was no time to waste. But as they rushed round to theatre, wheeling the patient with them, what shocked Della most was how good it sounded to hear Harvey automatically refer to them as a team.

CHAPTER SIX

IN THEATRE, HOURS LATER, Harvey sutured the abdominal drain in place and released the clamp, initiating the suction. The drain would remove any residual blood or peritoneal fluid from around the liver laceration, which he and Della had spent the past three hours patching, having slowly and steadily removed the offending tree branch and its splinters. With the exception of two additional nicks in the small intestine, which Della had meticulously repaired, this young man had been incredibly lucky. The internal damage could have been way more extensive and life-threatening.

'Are you happy for me to close?' Harvey asked Della, his back stiff from standing in the OR for so many hours.

Instead of the afternoon off they'd planned, they'd worked together on the complex surgery. Harvey was grateful for the second pair of eyes when it came to the areas of haemorrhage and the fragments of the broken branch they'd found in the man's abdominal cavity. He and Della worked together as if they'd been doing it for years, leaving all of their petty arguments behind, although not their sexual chemistry. Who'd have thought they could get along so well?

Della shifted a retractor, taking one last look at the repaired liver contusion. She wasn't going to be satisfied until she'd checked for herself, and Harvey respected her for that. As a consultant, he'd do the same. Della was an astute and thorough surgeon who didn't allow Harvey's slight seniority in years to deter her from making suggestions or questioning his technique.

'Looks as good as we can expect,' she said finally, her eyes meeting his over the top of her mask.

Harvey nodded in agreement and reached for a needle to close the abdominal wall layers one by one. 'Right, let's close him up. He's certainly not out of the woods yet, but we've done the best we can.' The biggest risk for the patient now that they'd stopped the bleeding was a postoperative complication, especially an infection. Hopefully the cocktail of IV antibiotics Della had started would help, but the young man's recovery would need to be closely monitored.

'I hear they've admitted three more casualties,' Della said, reaching for a second needle to help him close up the laparotomy wound. 'One head injury and two with multiple limb fractures who have been picked up by our orthopaedic colleagues.' She started her sutures at the other end of the vertical surgical incision so they would meet in the middle.

'Busy day,' Harvey agreed, glancing her way. 'We certainly had our hands full with this case. I'm grateful you were here.'

Before Fiji, he'd thought he'd known Della pretty well, but working so closely with her, not to mention their physical connection, was forcing him to take a second and third and fourth look. It was as if he was finally, after all this time, seeing the *real* Della, not the woman he'd spent twenty years avoiding looking at too closely in an attempt to manage his attraction. And it was freaking him out. Especially when she'd all but propositioned him this morning to continue their holiday fling until it was time to go home. Not that he'd needed any persuading.

'No,' she countered, flicking him a challenging look, 'I'm grateful *you* were here.'

Under his mask, Harvey grinned. Just because they'd slept together again, just because they'd agreed on a brief, physical fling, didn't mean their rivalry was completely over. And a part of him wouldn't have it any other way. He'd never felt bored in Della's stimulating, often challenging, company.

He dragged in a breath, his movements with the suture needle and forceps automatic. Now that their patient was stable and out of immediate danger, his mind wandered back to more pleasurable thoughts. There was no point trying to pretend that he was in control of their sexual chemistry, not here where they couldn't walk away from each other as they normally would. Having spent last night reacquainting himself with Della's body, Harvey would be fooling himself if he thought he'd be able to resist her while they were trapped together in Fiji. And as she'd said, a holiday fling was pretty harmless. They knew each other well. They were each invested in a future where they would see each other socially. They understood that when it came to relationships, they were complete opposites: she wanted one and he didn't. But a niggle of caution lodged in his brain. He didn't want to hurt Della. But she knew what she wanted, and for now, it was him; he'd be stupid to pass that up.

'But more compliments, Dr Ward,' Della said when he'd remained silent for a while. 'Careful, Harvey. There must be something in the Fijian water.' She glanced his way with that playful glint in her eyes.

Harvey chuckled, relieved that the events of last night, first their row and then spending the night together, hadn't affected their relatively new working relationship. That they could respect each other professionally after he'd been appointed to the Melbourne job gave him an enormous amount of satisfaction.

'You'll have my head swelling,' she went on, her movements as practiced as his as they sutured the wound. 'As you know, the Wiltons are such a high-achieving family, it's hard to feel as if you've distinguished yourself.'

Harvey looked up, her comment giving him pause, as if he should have realised she had self-doubts, as if they'd spent twenty years misunderstanding each other. He'd never considered it before, but it must have been hard for her, growing up the youngest in a family of medics.

'But you *have* distinguished yourself,' he pointed out. Was that why Della always seemed to have something to prove? Harvey could relate to that. For a while, during his teens, he'd been determined to show his absent mother what she'd given up on, a part of him striving to be a son of whom she could be proud, as if he'd hoped she'd want to renew their relationship. But the phone had stayed silent. He'd worked hard at school, earned a place at medical school, and become a leading surgeon in one of Australia's top hospitals, but some days, when his mind wandered to his mother, he still felt...inadequate.

'There's no question,' he added, dragging his thoughts from his own upbringing.

She shrugged. 'I guess. Although growing up in Brody's shadow, nothing I achieved was ever that extraordinary. And then, along came *you*.'

'Me?' Harvey tied off his last suture and cut the ends, his discomfort building.

Della looked up and nodded. 'Yes, *you*.' Her voice was playful, but he sensed she was about to offer information he hadn't known. 'I was just about to leave home for med school,' she continued, 'when Brody brought you home for the weekend that first time. Remember?'

'I remember I upset you with some immature comment about your boyfriend.' If she'd doubted her abilities back then, could that explain her sensitivity to criticism, especially when it had come from some guy she'd never met before?

Della ignored his reference and went on. 'You and Brody had just qualified, just started work as *real* doctors, and you were both insufferable. Strutting around, patronising me with warnings of how hard med school was, teasing me because I was moping over—' She froze. 'Oh, I can't even remember his name...'

'Oliver,' Harvey said, shame and regret hot in his veins as he recalled that weekend when he and Della had made such bad first impressions on each other and the part he'd played.

'Of course, Brody is such a great guy,' she continued as if he hadn't interjected, '*and* he's my brother, so I couldn't hate him for being better than me at everything. But you… You were fair game, I'm afraid.'

Harvey tried to find the humour in the story, but instead, his protective urges for Della fired. 'No wonder we hit it off badly,' he said. It shouldn't matter. The past was in the past, and they were just having sex. But the idea that she'd struggled to believe in herself among her competitive family, fearing she was second best to Brody, the idea of Della displacing her resentment for Brody onto Harvey, left him strangely flat.

Having closed the peritoneum and abdominal muscles, Harvey reached for a staple gun to close the skin. 'You know, I'm not sure if the appointment panel at Melbourne told you this, but you came very close to getting the job they offered me.'

Della stilled. Her eyes met his, full of questions. 'I appreciate you telling me that, Harvey, but I'm a big girl. I can live with second place, and I think they appointed the most experienced candidate at the time.'

Della's confidence in her abilities was attractive, but it was suddenly important to him that she knew of his regard. 'Credit where credit is due,' he said as he placed the final staple and reached for a dressing to cover the wound. 'Surgery is a competitive field. We're all vying for the same positions. Just because I got that job doesn't make me a better surgeon.' With the operation complete, Harvey gave the nod to the anaesthetist to wake the patient before stepping away and removing his mask and gloves.

'I know that—I'm heaps better than you,' she teased as they tossed their surgical gowns in the dirty laundry hamper.

'Well, I wouldn't go that far,' Harvey said as they left theatre to wash up. It was good to have their light-hearted banter back, but the more time he spent with Della, the more he realised that he hadn't really known her before, and he couldn't help but feel he'd missed out.

'You don't have to worry about me, you know,' she said, pausing at the sinks and turning on the taps to wash her hands. 'Despite the fuss I made over your job being rightfully mine, my ego wasn't really dented.' She looked up, met his stare. 'I was just in a bad place at the time, with the divorce. I needed a win. Any win. There's nothing better equipped to make you feel like a big fat failure than a divorce, trust me.'

Harvey reached for a wad of paper towels to dry his hands, a little lost for words that she'd confided in him. He was out of his depth with relationship advice, but he hated the idea that Della blamed herself for her marital breakdown. Harvey didn't know the details, but he was certain it wasn't Della's fault.

'Why would *you* be the failure?' he asked, defensive on her behalf.

'Oh, you know, because I should have seen it coming.' Della switched off the taps and yanked some towels from the dispenser.

Harvey struggled to find the right words. Della had never opened up to him before. 'Do you...want to grab a beer at Savu's?' he asked, wishing they were anywhere but at work so he could touch her, steal the kiss he'd waited all day for, make her smile. 'I'm happy to listen if you want to vent, although, as you know, relationships aren't my strong point.'

He didn't want to put his foot in it again. He watched doubt flit over her expression. He could understand that if she'd grown up feeling second best to Brody, the fact that she was now divorced, whereas her brother was happily married and a dad, might heighten her sense of failure.

'Don't worry, Harvey. There's no relationship to advise on. It's over. Forgotten.' She tossed paper towels in the bin and faced him with a brave face. 'I'm well shot of a man who, by the time we split up, had pretty much convinced me that his career was more important than mine, just because I wanted us to have a family.'

'What?' Harvey scowled, his flare of anger on Della's behalf hot and sharp. 'That's ridiculous.'

She shrugged, looking embarrassed. 'I know relationships are about compromise, but by the end, I felt as if he'd used my career as an excuse to put off talking about us starting a family, as if I couldn't possibly have both. As if I had to make a choice, a family or a career, but why should I? *He* didn't have to. *Brody* didn't have to. *You* wouldn't have to.'

'Why indeed?' Harvey frowned, shocked by the ferocity of his empathy. Had her doubts of being overshadowed by Brody bled into her marriage? Had smart and caring Della settled somehow for her ex's excuses? It was none of Harvey's business, but Della deserved so much better. She deserved someone who would raise her up, not tear her down. She deserved whatever white picket fence dream she chose.

They passed through a door and paused outside their respective changing rooms. It was after hours, their surgery clearly the last one of the day. The place felt deserted. Because it had been too long since they'd kissed, at least nine hours, not that he was counting, Harvey pressed his lips to hers, scooping his arm around her waist. She sighed, gripped his arms and returned his kiss.

His thoughts silenced, his body relaxing. Normally he kept people at arm's length, but with Della, because he knew her so well, because she was a big part of his life, because she'd opened up to him, he couldn't help but feel invested.

Before things turned too heated, Harvey pulled back. 'I know we haven't always seen eye to eye over stupid things,' he said, cupping her face, his thumb gliding over her cheekbone, 'but for the record, I think you're amazing.'

He needed to shut up. He was straying out of his comfort zone, but he cared.

'Thanks.' She blinked, clearly touched by his uncharacteristic praise. 'Another compliment. Aren't you scared by the potency of the water?' She smiled, playful, and his heart thumped erratically.

He *was* scared, but not of the water. The real Della, the one he couldn't escape here, the one he was uncovering like an archaeologist exposes a dig, was addictive. It was as if last night had broken some sort of internal restraint. He couldn't seem to keep his hands off her or stop thinking about her and the new things he'd learned.

'I guess you're not so bad yourself,' she said. 'But if we can't trust the water, perhaps we should go for that beer. I'm parched over here.' She was returning to humour as if she could sense the shaky ground on which he was standing and wanted to toss him a lifeline, or perhaps she was also wary of exposing too much. After all, this was about sex.

'Right. Savu's it is.' Harvey released her reluctantly. 'I'll meet you back here in five minutes.'

They parted ways, ducking into their respective changing rooms with matching goofy grins. Harvey removed his scrubs and headed for the shower, using the time to straighten his head. Just because he knew Della well, understood her dreams, had begun to see glimpses into her fears and regrets, didn't mean he could be her confidant. He'd been alone so long, he wasn't even sure he was capable of having more than a casual good time. He certainly knew nothing about the kind of lifelong commitment Della wanted.

Next time she looked sad over her failed marriage or compared herself to Brody, he would do well to remember that not only was he ill-qualified to give relationship advice, but he couldn't be responsible for her happiness. As she'd pointed out, when it came to a man like him, Della was smart enough to have zero expectations.

CHAPTER SEVEN

THE FOLLOWING AFTERNOON, sitting at the front of the two-person kayak with Harvey behind, Della sliced her paddle through the clear sapphire-blue water, a sense of relaxed contentment flooding her system. Maybe it was the warm sun on her back or the salt in her drying hair after their swim. Maybe it was the wonders of the coral reef marine life, the clownfish and the butterflyfish they'd seen while snorkelling. Maybe it was the thrill of beating Harvey back to the kayak in a swimming race and the steamy victory kiss she'd claimed when he'd finally caught up.

Della glanced over her shoulder and caught Harvey's eye. A goofy smile tugged at her cheeks. Maybe it was all those things combined with extreme sexual satisfaction.

'It's so beautiful here,' she said, steering the kayak back across the lagoon towards the white sandy beach of Tokuma Island, a picture-perfect tropical oasis accessible by water taxi from the main island and home to an adults-only holiday resort.

'Hmm,' he agreed, his superior strength propelling the kayak forward. 'Better late than never.'

Della nodded, a small part of her wishing they'd spent their postponed afternoon off in bed. She couldn't seem to get enough of Harvey Ward. The minute he'd arrived to pick her up for their island adventure that morning, she'd dragged him inside her bungalow and kissed him senseless. One thing had rapidly led to another. They hadn't even made it to bedroom this time, simply collapsed onto the sofa, tugging frenziedly at each other's clothes.

'I've had the best afternoon,' Della said, sighing happily as she recalled burying her face against the side of Harvey's neck and crying out her orgasm while Harvey had groaned, crushing her in his arms as he climaxed. Was there any better way to relax than sun, sea and sex? But no matter how hard she tried to compartmentalise their physical relationship, she couldn't help but enjoy Harvey's company—his dry sense of humour, his geeky encyclopaedic knowledge of most subjects, the playful challenge he brought to everything like a dash of spice, keeping life interesting.

Reminding herself to also embrace caution—

she couldn't get carried away and forget that he was still the same old Harvey—Della steered the kayak into the shallows. They climbed off and tugged it up onto the sand near the rental place—a palm-roofed shack filled with paddles and snorkel gear. They returned the masks and snorkels to the *used* bin and headed up the beach for the shade of one of the palm leaf umbrellas dotting the shoreline.

At her side, Harvey took Della's hand. She smiled over at him, the breath catching in her chest. She'd been nervous about spending too much time with him, but Fiji Harvey seemed like a completely different man to his Australian counterpart. He was fun and caring, and she had to constantly remind herself that he'd never actually been a boyfriend. His romantic gestures were merely a pretty irresistible form of sexual foreplay.

'I brought some snacks,' Harvey said as they sat on the warm sand. He opened his small backpack to reveal some crackers, a pack of nuts and two apples. 'We need to keep our energy up.' He winked, his suggestive smile sending Della's body molten.

'See, no matter how hard you try to hide it, you *are* a good guy,' she teased, opening the roasted almonds and popping one into her mouth, touched by his thoughtfulness.

'It's true.' Harvey shrugged and took a giant bite from one of the apples. 'That must be why Brody and Amy have asked me to be Jack's mentor for his naming day. I wasn't sure if they'd told you yet.'

He watched her carefully. Obviously *he knew* that Della had also been asked to mentor Jack, the equivalent of a godparent. Della nodded, not in the slightest bit surprised by Brody and Amy's choice. Harvey was Brody's best friend. Of course he would ask him to be there for his only son. But that meant, like it or not, she'd definitely see him again in three weeks' time. By then, their holiday fling would be a distant memory, although it would be hard to forget days like today, when they'd not only had great sex but also had fun and laughed together, making brand-new memories.

'I can't wait for Jack's naming day,' Della said, taking a long drink from her water bottle. 'As his aunt and his mentor, I'll have two excuses for cuddles. Don't tell my brother, but I might even steal him and smuggle him back to New Zealand.' She laughed, but a niggle formed a knot in her chest. She was happy for Brody and Amy, but newly divorced, it had been hard to hear their pregnancy news and not feel a massive pang of longing, as if yet again she was being left behind.

'I'm looking forward to it, too,' Harvey said with an easy smile combined with that hungry stare of his.

'Really?' she asked, trying to picture Harvey holding her baby nephew, who was coming up to six months old. Jack had one bottom tooth and an adorably gummy smile. 'You've never struck me as the kids type.'

Harvey glanced her way, his expression unreadable. 'I like kids just fine. Small, cute humans—what's not to love?'

Della's pulse pounded with excitement as she watched him polish off the rest of the apple. There was something sexy about the way Harvey ate. Of course, there was something sexy about his every move, but she'd never have guessed he'd be comfortable around kids. But thinking about Jack's naming day left her wondering if she and Harvey could successfully ignore their fling once it was over, as they had last time. The idea that they'd revert to bickering strangers doing their best to ignore each other left her unsettled. She didn't want that. Maybe they'd finally become friends once this sexual chemistry had run its course?

She watched a droplet of water trail a path down his toned and golden abs. Nope, having Harvey as a friend seemed unlikely. Or would they still hook up every now and then, before Della moved on to a new relationship?

'Contrary to what some people believe,' he said, distracting her from how exactly their relationship would work in the future, 'I even possess a heart.' He shot her a teasing glance, and stowed the apple core in a paper bag.

Guilt left her flushed. 'I guess we didn't really know each other very well before Fiji,' she said, lying down beside him on the sand, where he was propped up on his elbows. She rested one hand on his chest, brushing at the grains of golden sand that glinted on his skin.

'I guess we didn't,' he said, lying back and pillowing one bent arm under his head. 'I'm glad we finally got the chance to know each other better.' His other hand came to rest on hers, his intense stare shifting over her face.

Della's belly fluttered as if he'd hungrily scoured every inch of her bikini-clad body. She recognised that look, and his touch, no matter how innocent, never failed to turn her on.

'You know,' he said, falling serious, 'I *did* have a relationship once, a girlfriend, before I met you and Brody. I wanted you to know, because…you know, relationships aren't easy, for anyone.'

Della stiffened, gaped, completely at a loss for what to say. Her fingers stilled in his dark chest hair, the rapid thud of his heart under her palm telling her this was hard for him to confess. And was he reassuring her again because she'd told him how her divorce had made her feel like a failure? But Harvey...a girlfriend? He was *Harvey*. Never short of offers but always alone at couple times—Christmas, birthday celebrations, holidays.

'Did you love her?' she asked finally, her raging curiosity an uncomfortable gnawing in the pit of her stomach. Was that what he'd meant when he'd said being vulnerable with another person was a *brave gamble*? Had Harvey had his heart broken and subsequently turned his back on commitment? How had she never known this about him? And why should it matter? She wasn't jealous. It was just that the more time she and Harvey spent together, she realised that she didn't really know him at all.

As if he regretted the impulse to share this with her, Harvey sat up, rested his arms on his bent knees and looked out to sea. 'I don't know... maybe.'

Well, that was vague. The easy, laid-back vibe they'd enjoyed all afternoon while they'd swum and snorkelled the reef departed. That jealousy she'd denied a moment ago slid through Della's veins like fire. Harvey in love? A secret relationship he'd kept from her. Did Brody know?

'What happened?' Della softly asked, scared to pry but even more scared to miss this opportunity to know him better, because in light of his revelation, they seemed like strangers again. 'Did she break your heart?' Was that why he was slow to admit he'd loved this girl? Was that why he'd avoided relationships all these years? It seemed like an extreme reaction, but she didn't want to judge.

'Kind of...' He sighed, keeping his back turned.

'Well, I can understand why you'd be reluctant to confide in me,' Della said. 'After the way I've judged you in the past. If it's any consolation, I regret that now.' Della lay stiffly on the sand, shame holding her tongue. She'd assumed that he was happy with casual sex, but now it seemed that the reality might be much more complex. He *had* been in a relationship once. He'd probably loved someone and had his heart broken. Brody was right—Harvey *did* possess hidden depths.

'It's not that,' he said, turning to face her, his expression stoic. 'It's just hard to talk about. She died in a car collision aged twenty-two. She was a medical student like me. Her name was Alice.'

Della sat up, covered her shocked gasp with her hand, her heart twisting painfully at the tragic news. 'I'm so sorry, Harvey. I had no idea.'

'It was a long time ago.' Harvey shrugged, returned his gaze to the sea. 'Brody knew that I didn't like to talk about it. I know he's a know-it-all as a brother, but as a friend, he's very loyal.'

Della's mind reeled. She understood that Brody would keep Harvey's secret, but she wished she'd known this vital piece of information sooner. In context, it painted tortured Harvey in a whole new light. He must have really loved this girl. Were heartache and grief the reasons a younger Harvey, the man she'd first met and taken an instant dislike to in a love-hate kind of way, had played the field? Had loving and losing Alice had a profound effect on him, so he avoided further pain by avoiding commitment?

Della swallowed, her throat burning with regret and jealousy. 'Is Alice the reason that you don't date?' she asked in barely a whisper, some part of her needing to know if he was still in love with this woman. Still grieving. Still heartbroken.

'It's not that cut and dried,' he said, keeping his back to her. 'I didn't wake up the next day and make a conscious decision that I was done with relationships for good. It just kind of happened that way.' His shoulders tensed. 'We'd been together a couple of years,' he continued, his voice tight. 'And although it probably wouldn't have lasted, I was devastated to lose her like that, so…suddenly. So pointlessly.'

'Of course you were. Who wouldn't be?'

Della reached out and placed her hand between his shoulder blades. Yes, their relationship was about sex, and this Harvey, a complex man hiding a vulnerable side, was a stranger to her, but she couldn't help but comfort him the way he'd tried to do for her at Savu's last night after she'd admitted details of her divorce.

But why wouldn't it have lasted? She desperately wanted to ask, but maybe she'd pried enough. Instead, she pressed her lips to his sunwarmed shoulder, her eyes stinging with emotion. Everything she'd assumed about this man had shattered like glass. He wasn't arrogant and competitive; he was dedicated and driven. He wasn't carefree and single; he was protecting himself. He wasn't two-dimensional; he was complex.

'I guess when the shock and grief faded,' he went on, 'it seemed easier, less effort, to keep my relationships superficial. No need to tell a one-night stand about your sad past. I didn't want to talk about it anyway, even if someone had asked.'

Della caressed his shoulder, too emotional to say anything. Why hadn't *she* asked? Instead, she'd taken him at face value, ridiculed his choices and used him for sex. Twice.

'I focussed on work,' he said, shooting her a wry smile. 'Before I knew it, one year had turned into another and another. By the time five years had gone by, I'd developed casual dating habits—keeping it light and impersonal, having a good time and moving on—that didn't seem to have any downside.' He glanced over his shoulder. 'You know that saying—"if it's not broken, don't fix it"?'

Della nodded in understanding.

'Well, that encompassed my personal life.' He shifted, lay back down on his side, pulling Della down too. 'I guess I just never found a good enough reason to change,' he said, although Della wondered if he might be holding something more back.

He propped his head on one hand, and she mirrored his position so they faced each other in the shade of the umbrella. 'Because relationships are risky,' she said flatly, knowing all about the pitfalls of loving someone and having your heart broken. But whereas Della hoped to find love again in the future, Harvey had found the perfect solution to protect his heart—staying single. He'd never met a woman it was worth risking the status quo for, or he just didn't see that anything was lacking in his personal life, or he was happy with the sacrifice if it meant avoiding pain.

'Don't you ever get lonely?' she asked cautiously, looking down at their clasped hands where his thumb slid against her skin, raising goose bumps on her arm. She doubted she could do what Harvey had done, stay alone all these years. She loved being part of a couple, having someone to share things with, someone who just understood you. Until it went wrong…

'How can I be lonely surrounded by Wiltons?' he said with a small smile, distancing himself from the question and the heavy turn in the conversation.

Della couldn't blame him for putting up emotional barriers. She'd done the same last night when he asked about Ethan.

'So you see,' he said, a twinkle of humour coming into his eyes, 'I'm not heartless. I'm just stuck in my ways. Lazy.'

Della entwined her fingers with his, desperate to ask all the questions building inside. By avoiding long-term relationships, he was keeping himself safe, yes, but wasn't he also missing out on connection, on knowing someone on a deep level as much as they knew him?

'Lazy or scared?' she asked, looking up. She could fully relate to the latter. Putting herself back out there in search of a relationship, of the right man, often seemed too monumental to contemplate, but unlike Harvey, she didn't want to be alone forever.

'You're probably right,' he said. 'Although my

explanation puts me in a better light.' As if he wanted to draw a line under the topic, Harvey leaned close and pressed his lips to hers, the heated kiss almost enough of a distraction to end the conversation.

His hand rested on her waist, his tongue sliding against hers. Della sighed, turned on by his touch but still reeling from everything she'd learned about him in the past few days. It was as if she hadn't known the real Harvey at all, as if she'd filed him away in a mislabelled box to keep herself safe from her feelings, and now she needed to re-examine them in the cold light of day. No, there were no feelings beyond attraction and respect. Feelings had no place in their fling.

Pulling back, she rested her forehead against his, breathing hard. 'I understand the fear, you know, the emotional gamble of being vulnerable with another person. Why do you think I haven't bothered with dating since the divorce? I've had my fingers burned, and I'm in no rush to go through that again. It's as if my instincts, my judgement took a massive hit.' That part of her that hadn't seen her marital problems coming was terrified to let another person close, terrified to get it wrong, again. Although her time for meeting *the one*, for falling in love and starting a family, was running out. She'd be forty in two and half years.

'I can understand that.' His searching stare flicked between her eyes, so Della wanted to hide behind her sunglasses. He cupped her face. 'But you deserve to be happy. You deserve to have it all, Della, if that's what you want.'

Della nodded, her throat hot and achy. To be seen for the first time since her divorce, and by Harvey of all people... She *did* want it all, but having what she wanted wasn't straightforward.

'Knowing what you want is the easy part,' she said with a sad laugh, looking down at their clasped hands to hide her eyes from him. 'It's finding someone who wants the same as you that's tricky. I've already got that wrong once.' She didn't want to think about her ex, not lying here hand in hand with Harvey, when they were finally sharing something personal, when she felt so close to him. But now that she knew his reason for avoiding relationships, their differences were more obvious than ever. It wasn't that Harvey wanted to be single. It was that he didn't ever want the risk of a relationship, and to eternally romantic and hopeful Della, that was the most depressing thing she'd heard for a long time.

'It will happen,' Harvey said, an encouraging smile in his eyes. 'You have everything going for you—a great career, an awesome personality, this sexy body...' His smiled stretched, but then he sobered. 'Just don't settle for less than you deserve, okay?'

Della nodded, confused that Harvey, of all people, understood her so well. Had she compromised too much and settled with Ethan? Had she, over time, allowed her ex's dreams to eclipse and squash her own? It hadn't felt that way at the time, but by then end of their marriage, he'd changed. He'd sold her a fairy tale and rewritten the happy ending.

'You deserve to be happy too,' she said tentatively, too scared to know if he was still in love with Alice. 'What does that look like for you? Being alone forever?' Her pulse pounded so hard, she feared he might feel it in her fingers. This degree of emotional intimacy was uncharted territory for them.

'I don't think about forever.' He shrugged, his stare untroubled. 'I just know that right now, my life is good. I'm in control. Why would I mess with that?'

'Ah…the control freak again,' Della said, trying to make light of it even as her heart sank. She told herself she was disappointed for Harvey, because surely everyone wanted to be in love? To share their life with someone? To feel deeply connected to another human being? But maybe for Harvey, control of his emotions was more valuable. And a part of her could understand.

'Don't feel sorry for me,' he said, tugging on her hand and steering them back to playful territory. 'I do all right with ladies, as you know.' He winked, drew her close, captured her lips in another searing kiss that fogged her mind and silenced all her questions.

Bewildered by what she'd learned, Della surrendered to his kiss, her lips parting, their tongues gliding. There was no point stressing Harvey's choices. The two of them were there to have a good time, not to build a relationship, even a friendship. If nineteen years of casual sex hadn't helped him get over Alice, what chance did Della have in two weeks? He wasn't hers. He wasn't anyone's. If she became distracted by the real Harvey, the man she was coming to understand more deeply every day, she might forget to focus on their physical relationship. She might forget how they still wanted different things, and likely always would.

She gripped his biceps and lost herself, her body sliding closer to his until her breasts grazed his bare chest and their thighs touched. As their kisses built in intensity, she grew aware that she was only wearing a bikini and Harvey board shorts. They were on a public beach on an island popular with snorkellers. They might be in paradise, but they weren't alone.

Breaking away, she calmed her excited breathing. 'We should, um, head back. The last water taxi is at seven.'

Harvey nodded, sliding his legs from the tangle of hers with a wince. 'Just give me a second.'

She smiled, glancing at the bulge in his shorts. When he was ready, they gathered up their belongings and walked hand in hand towards the resort and the dock for the water taxi. As she sat snuggled into him on the boat, her back to his front and his arms around her waist, Della was stunned by how little she'd known Harvey before and how much they had in common beyond their jobs. This man, the dedicated doctor protecting his vulnerable heart, was way more dangerous to her than the carefree ladies' man she'd easily dismissed for close to twenty years.

But Della still wanted the future she'd been denied—love, marriage, a family. And when she finally overcame her fear, when she was finally ready to risk her heart again, she couldn't afford to make another mistake. Next time she fell in love, she needed to get it right.

CHAPTER EIGHT

THE NEXT DAY in the ED was hectic. Harvey and Della had no planned operations, so they'd split up to help the local doctors with the surgical admissions. Harvey had just finished seeing a six-year-old there on holiday with suspected appendicitis when a text came through from Della.

I have a patient who needs a second opinion if you're free.

Harvey washed his hands, his eagerness to reunite with Della leaving him jittery. Yesterday had been a big day. After their kayaking adventure at Tokuma Island, after he'd opened up to her about Alice's death and she'd hinted again at her regrets over her marriage, she'd spent the night at his bungalow. They'd wordlessly showered together, lazily washing the sand and salt from each other's body before falling into bed. They hadn't talked about their pasts again. It was as if they were each processing what they'd learned. The trouble was that by spending so much time with her, by discovering new things about Della, by constantly needing to touch her, Harvey was struggling to keep his emotions in check. He felt out of control, and that was a huge concern. Her words from the day before looped in his mind.

You deserve to be happy too... What does that look like for you? Being alone forever?

Distracted anew by the power of that question, Harvey went in search of Della. He'd never seriously considered it before, but now that she'd raised the idea, now that it was out there in his consciousness, he couldn't seem to put it out of his mind. Nor did he know the answer. Maybe he shouldn't have let Della in yesterday, but he'd wanted her to know that most people had relationship regrets, that she wasn't alone.

Harvey found Della in a nearby bay with an anxious-looking couple in their thirties. As always, his pulse banged at the sight of her, his fingers restless to touch her soft, sun-kissed skin, his lips eager for those passionate kisses that always escalated out of their control.

'Dr Ward,' Della said, her expression both apologetic and relieved. 'Thanks for coming. Mr and Mrs Beaumont would like a second opinion, and I told them you're Melbourne's top trauma surgeon.' Her stare carried questions, as if checking he was okay after his confession yesterday. But he'd rather she look at him with desire than pity.

'Only because they were too stupid to appoint you, Dr Wilton.' Harvey smiled at the patient, Mr Beaumont, who was lying on the stretcher, supporting his left arm in a sling.

Della was a compassionate doctor, a talented surgeon and a good listener. She would be a catch for any man. Harvey hated to see the threads of doubt she carried. Yes, she knew what she wanted, but she also felt that she'd compromised too much in her marriage.

'The Beaumonts are here on their honeymoon,' Della told Harvey. 'Mr Beaumont is a fit and healthy thirty-year-old who fell off a jet ski this morning travelling at approximately fifty kilometres per hour. He sustained a mild concussion on hitting the water and has an anterior dislocation of the left shoulder.'

Harvey listened as Della pulled up the shoulder X-ray on the computer, which clearly displayed the dislocation. She angled the screen so the newlyweds could also see the results. Harvey quickly examined the man's arm and then scrutinised the X-ray and read the report, in no doubt of Della's diagnosis. It was a standard case of shoulder dislocation, but some patients needed a second opinion. That didn't mean Harvey was better equipped to treat this patient than Della. He trusted her clinical acumen unreservedly. In fact, he realised with an internal jolt, he trusted her, full stop.

That was why he'd told her about Alice. But when had that change happened…?

'So I'm afraid, as Dr Wilton pointed out,' Harvey said, standing side by side with Della in solidarity, 'you have a dislocated shoulder. I agree with her diagnosis.'

Harvey glanced Della's way, hoping she saw his absolute faith in his stare. But standing close without touching her left him restless to drag her into his arms and chase off all her doubts. The same fiercely protective urges he'd experienced yesterday at the beach when she'd told him about her ex-husband flared anew now. What was going on with him, and how could she make him feel this way when he'd effortlessly avoided it for twenty years?

'The good news,' he added to Mr Beaumont, 'is that there doesn't appear to be any fracture or significant tendon or muscle damage, so you won't need surgery. But I concur one hundred percent with Dr Wilton's clinical assessment and the treatment she's suggested.'

Tearful, Mrs Beaumont dabbed at her eyes with a tissue and gripped her husband's hand on his uninjured side. Harvey could sympathise.

Of course the wife would be worried. No one wanted their honeymoon marred by injury, but these things happened when you came off a jet ski at speed. The man was lucky the injuries weren't more serious, particularly the concussion.

'Once we put the shoulder back in place,' Della said, her voice reassuring, 'and once the pain and swelling have gone down, you should make a full recovery. If you're happy for us to proceed, we can quickly pop your shoulder back into the joint. The sooner we do that, the less the risk of surrounding tissue damage. Why don't you two chat about it for a moment.'

Harvey and Della left the bay and moved a short distance away so they wouldn't be overheard.

'Thanks for sticking up for me so heartily back there,' she said, looking up at him with a curious smile, perhaps because in the past, when Brody teased her at family gatherings, Harvey had always kept quiet or joined in. If he'd known back then how Della's feistiness was a shield because she compared herself to Brody, how she felt the need to prove herself, how she considered her divorce in particular a personal failure, he'd have been way more tactful.

'Any time, Della.' Shame for how he'd behaved when he'd been focussed on keeping a lid on his attraction for Della coiled inside him. 'You know it's not personal—some patients just like to question everything.'

'Of course.' Della nodded, a flicker of amusement in her stare. Then she sobered and frowned. 'Are *you* okay?' she asked, glancing around the department to make sure they were alone. 'You know...after yesterday. You were gone when I got out of the shower.'

'I wanted to get in a run before work,' he said, shaking off the unfamiliar swarm of emotions that yesterday's confessions, both his and hers, had churned up. 'But I'm fantastic,' he said, staring intently. 'I had a great sleep and woke up feeling...energised.' He'd kissed her awake, as if reaching for her naked body next to him had become the most natural thing in the world, and he wanted her to look at him as she had when he'd pushed inside her and rode them both to orgasm. Would he still reach for her back in Melbourne? Would he crave the scent of Della's perfume on his pillow? Would he acclimatise to having an empty bed again? The idea was mildly depressing...

Della flushed and shot him a censorious look. 'I remember,' she said. 'No need to brag.'

Harvey reined in his smug smile. 'Shall I leave this to you?' he asked about the shoulder dislocation. 'You don't need me.' Although he'd somehow grown used to them working together. They made a great team. Another thing he'd have to get used to when he returned to Australia.

Della shrugged, her ego clearly undamaged. 'I think the wife just expected a prescription for some painkillers and to be sent on their way.'

Harvey bit his tongue, mildly insulted on Della's behalf that her skills had been questioned. A junior doctor could reduce a shoulder dislocation, whereas Della was an experienced consultant trauma surgeon.

'If you have a moment,' she went on, 'I could use your assistance. I prefer Matsen's traction to reduce a shoulder dislocation, and it's a two-person job.'

'Really? Matsen's?' Harvey asked about her choice of technique mainly because he enjoyed evoking the sparks of challenge in her eyes.

'Yes, Matsen's.' She smiled a mocking smile, clearly onto him and in no way intimidated.

'You don't use the Milch manoeuvre?' he pressed, questioning her to bring out the barely disguised amusement in her stare. 'That's what *I* prefer...' These days, since they were getting along so much better, they weren't sparring as much. Part of him missed it, and maybe Della did, too.

'Well, it doesn't surprise me that we're different,' she said calmly. 'But my technique is better. And it's *my* patient.'

Harvey grinned, glad to see Della wouldn't let him get away with anything, despite the fact that she might be starting to trust him too. After all, she had opened up about her ex. 'Then it's your call,' he said, happily yielding.

'Good. Matsen's it is.' She shot him a victorious look. 'Come on. That shoulder isn't going to right itself. I'm sure the Beaumonts want to get back to their honeymoon.'

Dutifully, Harvey followed her back to the bedside. A week ago, when Della and he only knew the superficial things about each other, they might have more fiercely argued the point on whose technique was better, although there were many. But it didn't matter. They both knew the important thing was to quickly put the head of the humerus back into the joint.

After some time to consider, the patient was happy to proceed with the treatment. With Mr Beaumont lying on his back and the bed lowered, Della and Harvey took up their positions opposite each other, Della taking hold of the injured arm and Harvey standing next to the man's opposite shoulder. Harvey gripped the ends of a sheet passed around the man's chest and under his affected armpit, while Della held his dislocated arm in position, bent to ninety degrees at the elbow.

'Ready?' she asked the patient, who nodded and then closed his eyes, squeezing his wife's hand.

Della held Harvey's eye contact, silently mouthing *one, two, three* so they were in sync. She leaned back, applying traction to the patient's bent arm, while Harvey pulled on the sheet, applying counter-traction in the opposite direction. With a slight pop, the dislocation reduced, and the patient released a long sigh of relief.

Della flashed Harvey a grateful and triumphant smile that made him want to kiss the living daylights out of her. Instead, he beamed. 'Good old Matsen's. Worked like a charm.'

Della carefully hid her smile, clearly trying to stay professional in front of the patient. They thought differently on many subjects, but when it mattered, they'd proved time and again this week that they could compromise. Would they remember that when they saw each other in the future, or would they revert to bickering over nothing? Had this fling in Fiji forever altered their relationship? Harvey hoped so. He didn't want to go backwards where Della was concerned. Did that mean he wanted to be her friend? *Friends* seemed inadequate after everything they'd shared. But he couldn't seriously be thinking they could be more than friends, could he?

'Who's Matsen?' Mrs Beaumont asked, confused, interrupting the disconcerting turn of Harvey's thoughts.

Della flushed and shot Harvey a disapproving glare. 'It's the name of the technique we just used to relocate your husband's shoulder. Dr Ward and I differ on most things, so we'd discussed our preferences outside.'

Funny how those differences of theirs seemed less important here in Fiji. Harvey excused himself to the couple, quietly addressing Della before he left the bedside. 'Don't forget we have that bilateral laparoscopic acromioplasty to get to.' The made-up medical procedure was their secret code for a coffee break.

'I'll be there shortly,' she said with a straight face, turning to the patient with instructions. 'You'll need to wear a sling for the pain, and to help the swelling go down. I'll prescribe you some analgesia for the discomfort, but an ice pack will help too. And needless to say—no more jet-skiing.'

Harvey headed to the break room and flicked on the kettle, the euphoria of working with Della eclipsed by the return of his unsettled thoughts for the future. He made hot drinks, coffee for him and tea for Della, and then crossed the corridor to the deserted doctors' office to check his emails as a distraction, which was where Della found him a few minutes later.

'Thank you for your help back there,' she said, coming into the room. 'And thanks for trusting my technique. I know it's hard for you to take a back seat, control freak that you are.' She pursed her lips playfully, but all Harvey could think about was kissing her. Maybe then he would remember that this was about sex, not friendship or…feelings. Because when it came to relationships, to more than a casual good time, he had no idea what he was doing.

'For you, I'm always happy to take a back seat,' he said, dipping his head closer and dropping his voice in order to distract them both. 'Especially when we're so good together, in and out of work.'

Della laughed, a tiny shudder passing through her body, so he knew she was thinking about last night and this morning, about their near insatiable physical need for each other. Harvey pushed closed the door before drawing her into his arms. 'Is it wrong that I find your bedside manner incredibly sexy?' Without waiting for a response, he pressed his lips to hers, groaning when she speared her fingers through his hair and deepened the kiss.

This was under his control. Feelings had no place in what they were doing. Harvey was most likely having a wobble because he'd opened up to Della about Alice yesterday. Letting someone that close felt...unnatural. But Della had a way of sneaking under his guard.

'It could be considered mildly perverted,' she teased, tugging his lips back to hers.

Harvey gripped her waist and pressed her up against the closed door, pinning her with his hips. 'How can I want you again?' he asked, his lips sliding down the side of her neck. 'I'm seriously concerned for my own health. I feel like that Aussie marsupial mouse, antechinus, that commits reproductive suicide, literally dying from sex-fuelled exhaustion.'

Della laughed, gasped, tilted her head, exposing her neck to his lips. 'Don't be so dramatic. You know very well that the ultraviolet in sunlight increases testosterone levels. You're just holiday horny.'

He laughed and she brought his mouth back to hers, her body writhing restlessly as his hand delved under her blouse to feel bare skin. Thank goodness he wasn't alone. They couldn't seem to keep their hands off each other. Forcing himself to pull back, he rested his forehead against hers. 'I didn't just lure you here for this, you know. I made you a cup of tea.'

'Thank you, but you can lure me anytime.' She kissed him one last time and then pushed him away. 'That being said, we have the entire afternoon of work to get through.' She wiped at his mouth, presumably at the traces of her lip gloss, and straightened her blouse. 'Are you going to Dr Tora's barbecue tonight? We could walk to his place together if you are. It's not far from the hospital, apparently.'

'I'd love to walk with you,' he said, reaching for her hand, his restlessness building now that she was no longer in his arms. Touching her had become a compulsion, one he was trying not to overthink. Their days in Fiji were numbered. With him back in Melbourne and Della returning to Auckland, the necessary break would happen naturally, and Harvey would surely shake off this feeling that, for the first time in twenty years, a relationship that went beyond sex might not be so bad.

'We'd better get back to work,' she said sheepishly. 'The ED is filling up out there.'

Harvey nodded, his hands reluctantly slipping from her waist. 'If I don't see you before, I'll call for you at seven tonight.'

'It's a date.' She smiled, and he felt instantly lighter. She opened the door and ducked out of the office.

Harvey lingered for a few minutes more, trying to straighten his head. Could he and Della really go back to their former relationship after sharing so much? Could he see her at Jack's naming day and not want her? Could he watch her date and fall in love again without being eaten alive with jealousy?

But what was the alternative? Trying to have more than a physical fling with Della would surely put important areas of his life at risk—his newfound truce with her, his friendship with Brody, his valuable place in the Wilton family. Was he seriously considering taking those risks, not to mention the personal risks to him: that powerlessness he detested so much?

Because if he wasn't careful, if he overstretched and tried to have more than a fling, he might hurt Della and damage his relationships with all of the Wiltons. With those stakes, Harvey had the most to lose.

CHAPTER NINE

LATER THAT EVENING, after a family barbecue at the beautiful beachside home of Dr Tora, Della and Harvey waved goodbye and set off for the stroll back to their hospital accommodation. As soon as they were out of sight of the older man's elegant wooden villa, Harvey reached for Della's hand.

She smiled, shuddered, his touch now familiar but still new enough to affect her entire body with tingles. Because for Della, what had begun as *just sex* was now way more complicated.

'You okay?' he asked, picking up on her strange mood as they headed along the sand. 'You seem a bit quiet.'

'I'm fine—a little tired maybe.' Della faked a big smile, too confused by the way she felt to say more. She'd never in a million years have predicted that her and Harvey's previously strained relationship would turn so harmonious and confusing. Working together, sleeping together, discovering new things about him; it was intense.

And now, where Harvey was concerned, she could no longer easily untangle her feelings. She only knew they were dangerous.

'That was a lovely night,' she said to take her mind off the rush of panic. She stepped close, holding on to his arm with her other hand so they could walk side by side along the beach. 'Watching you get thrashed at footy by Dr Tora's grandchildren was a particular highlight for me.'

Harvey smiled, and Della relaxed. She didn't want to drag the evening down with her solemn mood, nor could she explain herself anyway. It wasn't like she could tell Harvey that uncovering his *hidden depths* had changed how she saw him and cracked open the lid on feelings she'd spent years denying. She knew it was ridiculous, but a part of her, the part she was scared to examine too closely, wondered if, in another life, they might have stood a chance of something more than just physical. But Harvey didn't want more.

'That little wiry one kept cheating,' Harvey said, the humour in his dark stare setting off another cascade of longing in Della. 'I caught him literally moving the goalposts more than once.'

Della chuckled, although in truth, the sight of Harvey, playful and sporty, engaging with the group of differing aged kids had made her mouth dry with lust and something else. Fear.

Was she at risk of developing real romantic feelings for Harvey?

Her stomach tight with unease, Della clung to the lighter topic. 'I guess that's easily done when the goal is an imaginary line between two coconuts, but well done for being a good sport. I'm not sure Brody would have let them win. He's too competitive.'

And right now, as befuddled as she felt, she really needed Harvey to be rubbish with kids, rubbish at *something*, although if he'd sworn off relationships, he obviously had no burning desire to become a father.

'Speaking of kids,' he said, glancing her way as if he somehow knew the path her mind had wandered, 'it's Mother's Day tomorrow. Don't forget to message Mrs W.'

Della watched him curiously, her hormones firing once more. Harvey really cared about her mother. Why had she never noticed that before? It was as if, when it came to Harvey, she'd been walking around with her eyes closed.

'If you don't mind,' he added, pulling his phone from his pocket, 'I was going to send her this picture of us.'

Della took a closer look. They were standing together on Dr Tora's veranda with the sea behind them, smiling into the camera, looking tanned and relaxed, Harvey's head tilted in Della's direction.

'Of course not,' Della mumbled, shocked by the contentment she saw shining in her own eyes. Would her mother recognise it? Would Jenny Wilton have awkward questions for them when they were next all together for Jack's naming day? No, she too knew Harvey well enough to know that any sort of relationship would be the last thing on *his* mind. It should be the last thing on Della's mind too, but perhaps this fling had simply proved she was finally ready to move on and start dating again.

Della passed the phone back. Everyone looked happy on holiday, especially if they were also having oodles of awesome sex. Her look of contentment didn't mean anything.

'Do you always wish my mother happy Mother's Day?' she asked, surprised. It just occurred to her that Harvey rarely talked about his own mother. Della knew his parents were divorced, but she'd always assumed his mother must have died.

Harvey shrugged, slipping his phone back into the pocket of his shorts. 'Your parents are like family to me. Mrs Wilton is the closest thing I have to a mother. She's always been so warm and welcoming. I send her flowers on her birthday, too.' He shot her a smug smile, and Della's pulse fluttered at his thoughtfulness.

'You complete and utter suck-up,' Della said in mock outrage. 'Show up me and Brody, why don't you.' But her rampant curiosity flared into an inferno. 'What happened to *your* mother? I've never heard you talk about her.'

A week ago she wouldn't have dared ask him such a personal question. But she and Harvey had come a long way since that first day in Fiji. Now he was her first thought when she opened her eyes. His appearance brought excitement, not annoyance. With every day that passed, with every new revelation she learned, she felt their deepening emotional connection. Perhaps that was the problem. It was time to go home and leave their holiday and their fling behind… She swallowed that metallic taste of fear. It would be a relief to leave Fiji next week, so she could feel back to normal.

'My parents split up when I was eight,' Harvey said, stiffening slightly at her side. 'She wasn't around much after that.' He kicked at a seashell, sending it skittering along the sand.

Della held her breath, a knot forming under her ribs. Brody often said that Harvey didn't like to rake over the past, but there was obviously more to the story. 'But she's still alive?' Della gently pushed, wondering if his estranged relationship with his mother shaped him. How could it not?

He nodded, keeping his face turned away, his gaze trained on the ocean and the setting sun on the horizon. 'She visited for a while after she left my dad. But soon, her visits dwindled.'

Della's stomach clenched with empathy. Why? Surely she'd want to see her son? 'I'm sorry, Harvey,' she whispered. 'That must have been hard for you and Bill.'

Why had she never asked about his mother before? Why had she never bothered to scratch the surface of this complex man? Out of fear, maybe, because she'd been trying to keep her distance? Falling for twenty-three-year-old Harvey Ward would have been younger Della's stupidest move. If the timing had been right for them both when they'd first met, she suspected that she would have fallen hard.

He shrugged, but now that she knew the real man so much better, Della tensed, instinctively attuned to his vulnerability. 'I was lucky,' he said, almost as if persuading them both. 'I got to live with my dad. He's a great father who always made time for me.'

'I have a lot of respect for Bill,' Della agreed. 'But as a kid, you would have loved both your parents.' She couldn't seem to let this go, as if finally she'd caught a glimpse of the innermost layer of Harvey Ward. The missing piece of the puzzle that would put everything into perspective and maybe help Della untangle her conflicted feelings.

Harvey winced, and Della's heart broke for him. 'I was torn in the beginning,' he said simply, but she felt him stiffen. 'Being happy to stay with my dad felt wrong, as did begging for my mother to take me with her every time she visited and then left again.'

'That's a horrible position to be in.' Della blinked away the sting in her eyes, grateful for the failing light. 'No kid should feel as if they have to choose a parent.'

What had his mother's repeated abandonment done to intelligent, caring Harvey? He must have felt so confused. Yes, he was close to his father, but that wouldn't wholly make up for his absent mother. No wonder he'd kind of adopted *Mrs W,* as he affectionately called Jenny Wilton, as an honorary mother.

'In the end, my mother made the choice for me.' He turned to face her, a sad, bitter smile touching his lips and his eyes hard. 'By the time I was ten, she'd remarried a man who had two little girls and moved out of state. I didn't really hear from her again after that. She chose her new life, her new stepdaughters, over me.'

Della's chest ached, her sore heart racing. Harvey had grown up feeling rejected by the one woman who was supposed to always be there for him, to love him unconditionally with a mother's special brand of love. Had that abandonment strengthened his reaction to his girlfriend's sudden death, made him the self-confessed loner who didn't believe in commitment and love?

'I wish I'd known this sooner,' Della said, her world rocked by his confession and what it meant. Did he want to be alone forever, or was he, like Della, simply scared to risk his heart again because life had taught him that the women he loved disappeared or let him down, or chose someone else?

This past week, buffeted by revelation after revelation, she'd just about managed to cling to their carefree and casual sexual chemistry. But how could she keep her feelings for Harvey in check, knowing what she now knew? How could she fit him back inside that box where she was safe from the way he made her feel—as if they might actually stand a chance?

'I don't like to talk about it,' he said, his voice gruff. 'It's bad enough to remember how powerless I felt at the time, to admit how many years I spent pushing myself, trying to be a son she could be proud of in the hopes that she'd one day come back for me.'

Della squeezed his hand. 'I understand.' Of

course he would feel powerless, never knowing if or when his mother might visit, wondering if he'd done something wrong, grieving and confused. Driven, intelligent Harvey would hate feeling that way. And then history had kind of repeated itself when Alice too was suddenly and definitively ripped from his life. No wonder he chose to keep his relationships superficial after that to avoid the risk of being hurt again. Harvey liked to be in control, and there was nothing worse than love for turning your world upside down.

Della reeled as they walked in silence for a few minutes. But she couldn't stay quiet for long, not when Harvey's pain was palpable. When the real Harvey, scarred and battle-weary, called to her, because they had so much in common. When it would be so easy to fall for the man she was getting to know, but for one giant obstacle: he wasn't the right man because they still wanted different things.

'You know,' she said, gripping his arm, 'you're not powerless now. You said it yourself—your life is good. You're successful and hot and, despite trying to hide it from me for the past nineteen years, a really good guy. *I'm* proud of you, especially given I used to think you were just a jerk.' Della tried to smile, clinging to humour to keep things light, desperate to feel the way she used to feel about him, before they'd come to Fiji. With that Harvey, she'd known exactly what to expect. She'd known she was safe.

Harvey returned Della's smile, dragging her close and pressing a kiss to her forehead. 'I see the need to offer compliments is catching. Maybe we should get off this island before we fall madly in love with each other.'

Della stiffened, his joke falling flat. There was something about it she just couldn't find funny, as if one more revelation, one more day working at his side or night in his arms would push her over the edge towards deep, deep feelings.

'It's not magical water, Harvey.' Retreating to their usual banter, Della forced herself to remember that it had been twenty years since Harvey had so much as thought about a relationship, let alone love. His mother's rejection was as heartbreaking as his girlfriend's death, but whatever his reasons for staying single, it meant that Harvey was seriously inexperienced when it came to commitment. She might like, respect and empathise with him now, but she'd still be a fool to fall for a man with so little relationship history, who only wanted to be in control of his feelings. *She* wanted more, so much more.

'Phew, well, that's a relief,' he said, casting her a playful smile and slinging his arm around her waist, the subject closed.

Della walked at his side on shaky legs, glad to have the conversation back on lighter topics. She *wasn't* stupid. When she was ready to fall in love again, she needed a man who knew what he wanted, whose dreams of commitment and a family matched her own. She wouldn't make the same mistake—falling for the wrong guy—twice.

But later, just before she drifted off to sleep in Harvey's bed, her mind returned to the idea that, with the exception of him being so rusty when it came to relationships and having very good reasons for protecting his heart, Harvey ticked an awful lot of boxes.

CHAPTER TEN

THE NEXT DAY was Sunday. Harvey suggested a walk to Vatuwai Falls, the relatively remote waterfall Dr Tora had recommended to them the day before. They'd spent the past hour walking inland from the nearest village, holding hands when the width of the track through the forest allowed. Of course, with Della wearing her sexy denim cut-off shorts, which made her backside look great, single file also had its advantages.

'There it is,' Della called excitedly over the sound of tumbling water. She shot him an excited smile and rounded the final bend in the forest track ahead of Harvey, disappearing out of sight.

Harvey lengthened his strides to catch up, Della's enthusiasm contagious. But she made everything better, brighter, richer. They laughed together. He slept more soundly with her in his arms. She even made the workday pass quicker. What was he going to do without her back in Australia? And how had she sneaked so close that he'd opened up and told her about his mother?

'I'm going in,' Della said as he joined her at the edge of the water.

The falls were nestled in the shade of the island's lush rainforest, the pool beneath ten feet of cascading water, cool and inviting. And they had the place to themselves. Della dropped her backpack and took off her T-shirt and shorts to reveal her gorgeous bikini-clad body, her stare full of that familiar challenge that boiled his blood. Harvey's mouth, already thirsty from the heat of the day and the physical exertion of the trek from the car, dried further with longing. How could he want her again when they'd had sex at sunrise? How would he ever switch off this ravenous craving? How would he see her in the future and not want her the way he wanted her now?

It was crazy, but since they'd started to get to know each other on a deeper, personal level, since he'd seen her fears and insecurities and felt comfortable to open up to her about his past, he'd started to imagine things. Terrifying things. Things that took the control he loved and snapped it clean in two.

Could Della and he have something more than a sexual fling? Could she ever take him seriously? Could she ever want a man like him? Della dreamed of the whole fairy tale, and he was not only severely rusty when it came to feelings, he was also scared that he might be broken. Maybe it was just the magic of Fiji, the dreamlike bubble away from reality. Perhaps it was that until they'd been forced to spend time together, he hadn't really known the real Della at all, and it was just messing with his head.

'Careful,' he called as she gingerly traversed the rocks at the edge of the pool before stepping into the ankle-deep water. They were at least an hour's walk away from the nearest village and further to proper medical care. If one of them slipped, had an accident out here, they'd be in serious trouble.

'Come on, Harvey; it's lovely.' Della ignored his warning and waded into deeper water, the surface lapping against the tops of her thighs, wetting her coral-pink bikini bottoms. Before his brain could re-engage, she dived under the water and surfaced closer to the plunge pool at the base of the waterfall.

Harvey dropped his backpack next to hers and quickly removed his T-shirt and shoes. He was already wearing board shorts, so he followed Della into the pool, the shock of cool water on his skin a welcome reset to the fire she'd set in his blood. When the water reached his hips, he dived in and swam in swift strokes after Della.

'Keep up,' she said, turning onto her back and laughing.

Della was a strong swimmer—she'd told him it was the only sport Brody wasn't good at, because he didn't have the patience to train—and she loved to throw out challenges. Normally he was happy to accept them. But today, maybe because he'd told her about his mother last night, maybe because he'd been reminded how Della's family was also his, how he needed the Wiltons more than ever what with Bill's diagnosis, he was feeling exposed. Needing to get his hands on her to switch off that part of his brain focussed on reason and problem-solving, the part wondering if they could possibly work in the real world, when Harvey had abandoned the things Della wanted years ago, he powered through the water, catching up to her at the base of the waterfall. Della laughed, tried to get away, splashed him in the face.

She might be a stronger swimmer, but Harvey was faster. He snagged her around the waist, treading water as he dragged her nearly naked body against his, so she was all soft curves and slippery skin, taunting him with the things he couldn't have. Because soon, he'd have to give her up, give this up.

The minute they touched, Della back in his arms where she felt way too right, need roared through his blood. 'You always keep me on my toes, do you know that?' He dipped his mouth to hers, captured her smiling lips and kissed her.

She draped her arms around his shoulders and kissed him back, her lips parting, her tongue sliding against his so his arousal flickered in his shorts. 'Well, just because you like to be in control, we can't have you growing complacent.' Laughing, she wriggled free of his arms and kicked away.

Complacent? How could he ever feel settled around Della? She made him unstable, as if he was spinning at the centre of a whirlwind, caught between opposing emotions—fear that he could never be what she needed and an almost overwhelming desire to let her in anyway. But he'd spent twenty years keeping people, including Della, out.

Needing her touch to dampen some of the panic, Harvey caught her again, gripping her waist. 'No chance to be complacent with you around,' he mumbled against her lips, stealing another kiss. To douse the heat they generated when they touched and to pay Della back for the splash to the face, Harvey kicked his legs, guiding them both under the cascading wall of water. The force and shock of the water hitting their heads broke them apart, gasping.

On the far side of the falls, Della laughed,

reached for his shoulders and kissed him playfully. 'You always have to win, don't you?'

'Of course.' He grinned, his stomach hollow. There was one aspect of his life where he hadn't excelled: relationships. Even if Della wanted more than these two stolen weeks in Fiji, with him of all men, was he capable of giving her more than sex? He didn't want to let her down or cause her pain. She'd been hurt enough in the past, and hurting her would mean disappointing, possibly losing, all the Wiltons. But could he really walk away, knowing that this attraction between them had always been there, knowing that he would see her again and again, knowing that now he had nowhere left to hide? She knew all his shameful secrets.

She kissed him, her tongue surging against his as her legs wrapped around his waist under the water. Her bikini-clad body scalded his skin, driving him from memories to the present. Harvey gripped her waist, his toes touching the rocky bottom of the pool. Behind the waterfall, the sunlight was dappled, and the natural pool of shoulder-high water extended into a cave carved from the rocks of the overhanging cliff. Some primal urge shifted through him, a feeling that they might be the only two people on the planet. Nothing seemed to matter beyond how her touch, her kisses, her saying his name made him feel…invincible.

'Why can't I keep my hands off you?' he groaned, growing harder inside his swim shorts as she dropped her head back, exposing her neck to his kisses.

'I know what you mean.' She gripped his waist tighter with her thighs, her breasts bobbing on the surface of the water, their creamy curves teasing him, as if begging for his touch, his mouth. Harvey cupped one breast, his hand sliding down her bikini top and raising the nipple to his lips.

'Harvey…' She sighed and slipped her fingers through his wet hair, releasing her hold on his waist so she slid a little further down his hips.

The heat of her bathed his erection through his shorts. He was struggling to think again, his only instinct to bury himself inside her and chase the mind-numbing oblivion that was never far away when they touched. If he could focus on this, on pleasure, for just a few more days, surely his perspective would return once he was away from the temptation of Della.

Harvey untied the top of her bikini so the cups fell. He switched sides, his grip on her waist tightening as he laved the other nipple. He looked up. Della was watching him, her eyes heavy with desire.

'I want you all the time,' he said, turning them around and backing up against the rocky ledge at the edge of the pool so he could hold her there with his hips. 'What are we doing to each other?'

'I don't know, but let's not stop yet,' she said, gasping when his hand slid between her legs and inside her bikini bottoms.

He was out of control for her, a rage of hormones and terrifying feelings. Fear gripped his throat. What if this all-consuming need for each other didn't fade once they returned to their respective lives in Australia and New Zealand? What if a part of him always pined for Fiji, for Della? What if seeing her back in the real world brought the nice, neat life he'd constructed for himself crashing down around his head? What if she was the only person who could fix it, but she didn't want him?

Before his thoughts could disappear down that blind-ending tunnel, Della slid her hand between their bodies, inside his shorts, and cupped his erection, massaging him in her tight fist so his mind blanked. Harvey dragged his mouth from hers, the last thread of reason strung taut to the snapping point. 'We don't have a condom.'

'I'm okay without it if you are,' she said, kissing the side of his neck while she continued to stroke him under the water.

Harvey groaned, capturing her lips once more.

They trusted each other. Knew each other. Neither of them would put the other at risk. Because he was consumed by desire, because she was looking at him as if he could give her everything she needed, Harvey untied one side of Della's bikini bottoms so the fabric slid away from between her legs.

She braced her arms around his shoulders as she sank a little lower, her stare holding his. 'I want you, Harvey.'

Triumph rocked him. He gripped her waist and pushed inside her, the heat of her fanning the rampant flames in his belly. Could she want him for more than sex? Could he give her what she deserved, what she craved? Commitment? But what if he failed, let her down, ruined things for them and for himself?

'Yes,' she hissed as he filled her, her lips parted on her soft gasp, distracting him from thoughts that had no place in what they'd agreed to: a fling.

He cupped her face, bringing her mouth back to his, pressing his tongue against hers, overtaken by an uncontrollable sense of wildness to focus only on this physical connection they'd found and moulded into something unfamiliar but so meaningful.

'Don't stop,' she said when they parted for air. She spread one arm and clung to the rocky ledge at her back while Harvey gripped her waist under the water, held her close to the rhythmic thrust of his hips.

'You're beautiful. I've never wanted anyone this much,' he choked out, watching arousal darken her eyes. 'You know I've always felt this way about you, don't you, since that first time we met?'

She gasped at his honest declaration, something in her stare telling him she too had denied their attraction. But there was no point hiding it. She made him crazy and always had, this possibility there between them since the start, as if waiting for the time to be right. But was *right* enough? As soon as Della was ready to date, she'd be looking for *the one*. Whereas Harvey was so far behind when it came to relationships, he might never catch up. They might never be on the same page. What if he tried and failed?

Because he didn't want to think about where that would leave him once they returned to normality, Harvey dived for her breast, raising it to his lips and sucking. Della cried out, one arm around his neck, holding him close.

'Yes, yes,' she moaned, so he picked up the pace, driving her higher, even as he fought off his own release. He could give her this, give her a part of himself he hadn't given anyone in twenty years. He'd let Della in emotionally. It was no wonder he felt bombarded by unfamiliar impulses.

'Della…' he groaned, his hips jerking erratically, faster and harder, his need for her boiling over.

She gasped, her fingernails digging into his shoulder as she shattered in his arms, holding him so close as her orgasm crested that all Harvey could do was crush her to his chest, bury his face against her neck and follow with a harsh cry.

'Are you okay?' he muttered, his lips against her skin, as he held her tight and came down from the high.

She nodded, retying her bikini top at the back of her neck. Slipping from her body, he helped her retie the bottoms, his insides trembling. What was she doing to him? And how would he return to his solitary life when he'd allowed her so close he feared she might be able to see through him as if he was made of glass?

Silently, they swam back under the waterfall to the main pool, holding hands as they waded ashore. Harvey glanced her way as they sat on the rocks in a shaft of tree-dappled sunlight to dry off and rehydrate. Was she, like him, moved by the intensity of what they'd just done? Was he being a fool to think she could ever take him seriously when it came to more than sex? Della was a practical, intelligent woman who knew exactly what she wanted. Could he ever be enough?

'Just to reassure you,' she said, leaning against his arm, 'because you've gone suddenly quiet—I'm on the pill. No need to worry about an unwanted consequence.' She looked up at him, the way she'd looked at him last night when he'd told her about his mother, as if he finally made sense.

'Thanks for the reassurance.' Harvey snagged her hand, raised it to his lips and pressed a kiss there. 'But I was thinking how we only have a few more days left, and how it will be extra hard to leave Fiji this time.' Because as soon as the real world encroached, they would be over. Did she still want that? Was there any part of her that wanted to see where this could lead?

She nodded, releasing a small shuddering sigh. 'I know what you mean.' She smiled at him, her expression relaxed. 'Best holiday ever.'

Harvey pulled on his T-shirt, needing to be less exposed. 'But you still want a baby, right?' he said, some inexplicable force in control of his words. 'Just not mine, obviously.' His gut twisted. With fear or some foreign ache? But he wanted Della to be happy, even if he couldn't be the man to make her so.

Della stilled, glancing over at him as if he'd asked some sort of trick question that required a considered answer. 'I do,' she said, looking down at her feet, flexing her toes in the water. 'But perhaps when I'm ready, I'll... I don't know...go it alone. Use a sperm donor. After all, I'm nearly thirty-eight. My time for finding Mr Right is running out.'

Jealous at the idea of Della with another man, Harvey pressed his lips together. Her lifestyle choices were none of his business. He certainly wasn't qualified to be the man of her dreams. It had been many years since Harvey had allowed himself to think about wanting a family. But would she truly be content to go it alone?

'That's certainly one way to go,' he said, keeping his voice light, although his throat burned. 'But isn't the adoring husband a crucial part of your dream life?'

Could he bear to watch Della walk down the aisle again now that they'd become...not friends exactly. In fact, there was no label for what they'd become. But for Harvey, it was the most meaningful connection he'd ever had. Why else would he have confided in her about his mother's abandonment? Why else was he constructing wild and improbable imaginings where he was a different man, a man worthy of Della? Especially when those imaginings put a huge part of his life—his valued place in the Wilton family—at risk.

'He was crucial...' Della rolled her eyes, looking mildly embarrassed. 'But I've kind of had my fingers burned. Maybe pushing so hard for a family was what scared off Ethan. Perhaps it's better to have part of my dream than to push for it all and end up with nothing again.'

Pricks of unease tensed Harvey's shoulders. 'Didn't he know you wanted a family before he proposed?' If Ethan had known the first thing about Della, surely it was that she'd always wanted to be a mother.

'Of course he did,' Della said, ducking her head so he could no longer see her eyes. 'But obviously he wasn't ready, or I asked for too much and ended up losing everything.'

Harvey gripped her arms, turning her to face him, his heart racing. 'Why shouldn't you have everything you want? It's not that you asked for too much, it's that Ethan sold you a lie or said one thing and then changed his mind.' His protective instincts built to a frenzy. He didn't want Della to ever doubt herself, or be scared to risk another relationship, scared to trust her judgement.

Despite being out of his depth, Harvey cupped her chin and raised her gaze back to his. 'Don't make that about you, when it was clearly his issue. You shouldn't have needed to convince him, Della. He should have understood your dreams and supported them. That's the prom-

ise he made when he married you. I was there;
I heard the vows.'

Della stared, speechless, blinking up at him.
Then she dropped her gaze. 'Marriage is complex, I guess...' She shrugged, a small, vulnerable smile on her lips. 'Despite the way Brody
makes it look easy.'

Harvey winced, hearing the hint of dismissal
in what she left unsaid. Of course Harvey had
no right to offer advice, knowing so little about
commitment and nothing about marriage. She
knew it. He knew it. Just because they were good
together, just because he'd started to wonder if
they had a future together, didn't make him some
sort of instant relationship guru.

'You're right,' Harvey said, reaching for his
towel to dry his legs. 'I'm the last man in the
world qualified to give relationship advice. I'm
not even sure I'm capable of being in one after
avoiding them all these years.' He shoved his feet
into his walking boots, withdrawing because he
was so obviously out of his depth, and she could
see right through him. She wanted a husband,
a baby, and he was ill-qualified to make her the
promise of even a real date.

'Maybe you're right to go it alone,' he added,
stowing his towel in his backpack. 'Why wait
around for some perfect guy to sweep you off
your feet? If you want a baby, you should have

one. Cute tiny humans. What's not to love?' Harvey shut his mouth. He had no idea what *he* wanted. But the idea of Della being a solo parent was almost as unsettling as the idea of watching her date men who were better qualified than him to be in a relationship.

Feeling powerless again, he reached for her hand and pulled her to her feet. 'Come on. Let's head back to the car. It's getting late.'

Eyeing him with curiosity, Della dressed and pulled on her backpack. They set off along the track through the forest, hand in hand once more. Harvey took some deep breaths, willing the storm inside his chest to abate. He needed to be careful. His thoughts, his imaginings were writing cheques he wasn't certain he could afford. He was the last man on Earth who should make Della any sort of promise. In a few more days, and they'd be back to their real lives. All he needed to do was silence the crazy possibilities in his head, enjoy the rest of their time together and try to ensure that their new close relationship survived once they'd each moved on.

CHAPTER ELEVEN

MONDAY MORNING, the day after their trek to Vatuwai Falls, Della awoke to find Harvey's note on her pillow.

Gone for an early run. See you at work x

She smiled, her heart fluttering with longing but her head slamming on the brakes. She headed for the shower, mulling over the intense conversation from the day before, when they'd talked about babies and her marriage and her dreams to have it all. It must have been her imagination, because Harvey had seemed...wistful? But she'd likely still been high from the way he'd touched her under the waterfall, as if he had no choice. The way he'd consumed her with his kisses and that hungry stare as he'd pushed inside her body. The way he'd confessed to always wanting her that way.

But that was just sex. Attraction. She'd felt it too, simmering away between them all these years. So why was she torturing herself with rumination when he'd also soon after warned her that he wasn't capable of being in a committed relationship? Just because she understood his heartbreaking reasons for being single didn't change the fact that he was essentially a relationship virgin, and Della was a veteran with one failed campaign, next time searching for *the one*. And she couldn't afford to get it wrong again.

Quickly dressing, Della drank a cup of tea and dried her hair, her feelings a confused mess. But feelings, whatever shape they took, were irrelevant where Harvey was concerned. Anything beyond respect and lust was ridiculous. This was *Harvey*. Single for the past twenty years Harvey. Even if, through some major transformation, he wanted to temporarily continue their fling when they left Fiji, not only was it was physically impossible—he lived in Australia and she lived in New Zealand—it was also a huge risk to Della. If she was sleeping with Harvey, she wouldn't be dating someone else, someone who wanted to settle down, to fall in love and start a family. That was a lot to give up for *just sex*.

Trying and failing to forget about Harvey, Della arrived at the hospital. She'd barely made it to the department of surgery when an urgent call came through. She hurried to the ED, finding Harvey just ahead of her in the corridor, his hair still damp from a shower.

'What do we have?' Della asked, meeting his stare as a flurry of butterflies shifted inside her.

'Suspected stabbing, I think,' he said, shooting her a secret smile and then switching on his game face.

That's what Della needed to do. Pretend she had everything under control. Then, maybe by the time she arrived home, it would be true. Her feelings would shift into perspective and life would go back to normal, without Harvey.

Seema, the ED nurse, met them inside the resuscitation bay. 'We have a fifty-six-year-old man presenting with acute shortness of breath,' she said, handing over the ambulance report. 'Paramedics found what looks like a stab wound in his left chest wall. Erect chest X-ray results should be through any second.'

Della and Harvey rushed to opposite sides of the patient. The man was conscious, pale and sweaty and unable to talk for breathlessness. On autopilot, Della checked his vital signs on the monitor and then reached for a tourniquet. While Harvey palpated his abdomen and listened to his chest, Della drew blood from the man's arm.

'Reduced breath sounds on the left,' he told her and then added to Seema, 'I need a chest drain, please, and an urgent echo. We need to make sure the knife hasn't penetrated other structures in the chest.'

Keeping one eye on the blood pressure monitor, Della quickly labelled the blood tubes for the lab, passing them to a hospital porter. 'I've ordered a cross-match for blood transfusion,' she informed Seema. 'Have the police been called?' This obviously wasn't a self-inflicted wound.

The nurse nodded and set about replacing the empty bag of intravenous fluid feeding the drip in the patient's arm. Harvey tapped at the computer keys, bringing up the digital chest X-ray, which showed a white-out of half the left lung, indicating the presence of blood in the chest.

'Haemorthorax,' he confirmed, glancing at Della. She joined him at the monitor and took a closer look, scouring the image. 'Looks like some free air there under the diaphragm, too.' It was subtle, but free air in the abdominal cavity suggested a puncture of the stomach or intestine. 'The knife must have passed through the diaphragm.'

Harvey gave a nod, clearly on the same wavelength. Stabbing injuries to the chest, while clearly life-threatening, could also enter the peritoneal cavity and damage abdominal organs. And given the man's blood pressure was dipping dangerously low, the best way to assess trauma to the spleen, liver or kidney was an exploratory laparotomy. There was no time to hesitate.

'I'll call theatre and the anaesthetist,' Della said, reaching for the phone. 'You insert the chest drain.' The sooner they operated, the sooner they could stop any haemorrhaging and repair the perforation to the gut.

With the man booked in for an emergency laparotomy, Della quickly washed up, pulled on sterile gloves and joined Harvey on the patient's left side. Harvey swabbed the skin of the man's left chest wall and administered some local anaesthetic. Chances were there was a partial collapse of the lung along with blood inside the chest cavity. The chest drain would drain the blood and help the lung to re-expand. While Harvey carefully but expertly inserted the chest tube to drain the blood and escaped air, Della explained the man's injuries to him and consented him for theatre.

Thirty minutes later, with the patient anaesthetised and his abdomen opened up, Della found the puncture to the stomach along with a two-centimetre laceration of the liver.

'There's the hole in the diaphragm,' Harvey said, repositioning the suction to clear the operative field of blood.

'Thanks,' Della said, reaching for a suture.

'Let's sew up the liver first. Then we'll tackle the stomach.'

Harvey turned to the scrub nurse. 'Can we have a laparoscope, please?' He turned back to Della. 'We can take a look inside the chest before we close the hole in the diaphragm, make sure the pericardium is intact.'

'Good idea.' Della nodded, her eyes meeting his for a second. The echo had shown the heart and the sack around it appeared normal, but it didn't hurt to double-check while the patient was under anaesthesia.

Without getting in each other's way, they repaired the liver laceration and stitched up the stomach perforation. Operating together had become so intuitive now, Della worried that she might forget how to do it alone when their time in Fiji was over. But she couldn't rely on Harvey for anything. Reality was calling. By the end of this week, he'd go his way and she'd go hers, and this, *them*, would be over.

She waited for the rush of relief, but it didn't come. Perhaps that was simply because they still had one more test to get through before they were truly out of the woods when it came to moving on: Jack's naming day. She would see Harvey again in a couple of weeks. It was hard to believe that she wouldn't want him still. But indulging would only delay the inevitable, and she'd be foolish to endlessly pursue a dead end. She couldn't have Harvey forever, so it was best to make a clean break after Fiji. To try and switch off the constant need for him. To fill her thoughts with something other than Harvey and how he made her feel as if she'd been alone for long enough, that as long as she kept her eye on the prize, she *could* achieve her dreams.

An hour later, with the surgery complete and the patient headed to the surgical ward, they de-gowned, washed up and headed for the staff room.

'I need tea,' Della said, flicking on the kettle. Maybe it was a good idea to start weaning herself off Harvey now, before she became any more attached.

Harvey passed Della the tea bags, his stare distracted. 'Let's sit down for a few minutes. I have something to tell you.' He busied himself with making black coffee, his expression serious so Della's nerves fluttered in her chest.

'Oh, oh. That sounds…ominous.' Della added milk to her tea, her mind unhelpfully filling in the blanks. Was he flying home early as she'd teased that day they'd agreed to their fling? Given that she'd literally just decided to start a controlled exit, that shouldn't matter, but her stomach took a sickening dive nonetheless, telling her she was already in trouble.

'I think it's good news,' Harvey said, leading the way to two comfy armchairs in the corner of the staff room.

'What is it?' Della asked impatiently, taking a seat.

'I checked my work emails this morning.' Harvey settled into the chair next to her and placed his coffee on a side table. 'Dr Jones, one of my senior colleagues, has announced his retirement.' His stare met hers, so she saw a flicker of excitement there. 'They'll be appointing his replacement, if you're interested.'

His tone was casual, but Della stilled, her heart racing with both a surge of excitement and a greater sense of panic. Before Fiji, before she'd slept with Harvey again, before she'd seen the other side of him, a job back in her native Melbourne doing what she loved would have been a dream come true. But now...the idea of working in Harvey's department came with extra considerations. Could she see him every day and get over him, over this fling, at the same time?

'You don't like the idea,' he said, his voice flat.

'It's not that.' Della touched his arm. 'I'm thinking,' she hedged, her mind racing as fast as her pulse. 'Has the job even been advertised yet?'

'Not yet,' Harvey confirmed, ignoring his coffee while he observed her intently. 'But there have to be some perks when you're sleeping with the head of the department.' He flashed her a cheeky wink. 'I'm giving you advanced warning, before the job goes public.'

'There's no guarantee I'd get it, of course,' she mumbled, unable to meet his stare. Maybe the fact that a big part of her loved the idea was reason in itself to be cautious. Yes, their time in Fiji had proved that when it came to their jobs, they could get along just fine. But that was with a set expiration date for the end of their fling. It would be a very different story if their physical relationship limped along back in Melbourne, until one of them—Della because she wanted more, or Harvey because he didn't—broke it off. And what then?

Could she continue to take the only part of him on offer, sex, knowing he was too scared to ever consider having a real relationship? Could she work in the same department as Harvey every day and watch him return to his single life? Could she see him socially with her family and still manage to keep her own feelings at bay? Because she could not fall for Harvey Ward. They wanted different things. She'd be humiliated again. Hurt. And she'd only have herself to blame for making the same mistake twice.

'Hmm…' she offered, 'perhaps I'm just too tired to think straight. We have been living on very little sleep for a week.' Della tried to smile, but it felt like a grimace. 'Perhaps we should sleep alone tonight and catch up.' She felt sick. Suddenly she had no idea what she wanted, but some distance, some time away from Harvey to think, might help.

'Of course…' he said, concern and guilt hovering in his stare. Then he frowned, glanced down at his hands. 'I'll be honest. I thought you'd be a little more enthusiastic about the job. After the hard time you gave me three years ago, I assumed moving back to Melbourne was still something you really wanted.'

'It *is* something I want,' Della said unconvincingly. 'I'm just considering all the implications.'

'What implications?' His frown deepened.

'You know…' Della squirmed. 'Us, working together.' There was a lot to think about. It wasn't a decision she could rush, not if she hoped to protect herself in the process.

'We've managed to do that successfully for over a week, Della.' Harvey shrugged, a flicker of hurt in his eyes. 'Why would Melbourne be any different?'

Della swallowed. That was exactly her point— it *wouldn't* be any different. With the exception of their fling being over, everything would be the same. Harvey would still be avoiding relationships, because on some level he was scared to be vulnerable after being abandoned by his mother and losing Alice. And Della wanted a relationship, but would still be terrified to pin all her dreams on another person in case she got it wrong again. But the fact that Harvey was suggesting them working together would be easy told Della exactly where his head was. For him, it was straightforward. The fling would be over, business as usual, no problem. Whereas Della already suspected she'd take longer to adjust, that her feelings, her desire for him, would take time to switch off.

Hoping the wild flutter of her pulse wasn't obvious, Della breathed through her fear and met his stare. 'It's not that we *couldn't* successfully work together, Harvey. It's just… It would be intense after…you know…everything we've shared here. It will take some time to adjust to going back to what we were before. That's all.'

She couldn't bring herself to call them friends. She had a sneaking suspicion that Harvey would always be tempting. She'd known going into this fling that it was temporary, but now that it was almost over, now that she understood him, now that she saw he might be too broken to allow himself to be happy, to believe he was loveable, there was a part of Della that couldn't help but wonder *what if*?

What if he could see that he was worthy of

being loved? What if he overcame his fear and gave a real relationship a shot? What if she and Harvey *could* work?

'I think we could make it work,' he said, as if reading her mind. But where she was talking about a relationship between them, he meant them working together in the same department.

Della almost laughed at how out of sync they were, but instead nodded vaguely, her fatigue weighing heavily. Of course she was so much more invested emotionally than Harvey. He'd spent twenty years holding people away, whereas she wore her *heart on her sleeve*, as he'd said. Just because he'd told her about Alice and his mother didn't make Della special. He was still putting up emotional barriers, and if she wasn't very careful, she'd make a fool of herself and get hurt.

'I'd hate our fling to be the reason you didn't apply,' he pushed, making it sound so easy, so cold and clinical. 'I know how much you miss being close to your family.'

Della nodded, her heart sinking. That was Harvey—his mind on the fling, confident that when it was over, he'd just slip back into his single life. But he'd warned her that he was no good at relationships. He'd abandoned messy emotions years ago, because they made him feel powerless. If she'd ignored the obvious signposts, that was *her* problem.

'Well, I'll definitely look out for the job ad,' she said. 'Thanks for the heads-up.'

'Great,' he said, sounding less certain than before.

Della swallowed the lump in her throat, glugged her tea and pasted on a bright smile she was far from feeling. He seemed merely worried about a bit of workplace awkwardness, given the amount of sex they'd had. He hadn't mentioned them continuing to see each other after Fiji, but then, what did she expect? And was she really going to miss out on her dream job again because of Harvey, when all she needed to do was put this fling behind her as easily?

'I might head back to the emergency department,' Della said, standing. 'See what's happening before I call it a day. You finish your coffee.'

He nodded, clearly bewildered, and she fled, needing some distance. As she walked, she gave herself a stern talking to. Clearly Harvey saw no problems with them working together, because he fully intended to return to his old life. It was only soppy, romantic Della who was overthinking it with improbable what-ifs.

Even if by some miracle, Harvey wanted a real relationship, when it came to commitment, he was beyond rusty. Della couldn't afford to carry him while he tried a relationship on for size. Nor, with time to build her dreams running out, could she afford to be wrong again about anyone, including Harvey.

Harvey walked into the ED, guilt and confusion still knotting his insides. Della *had* looked tired. Was his constant need for her selfish? Their time together in Fiji had been intense. Perhaps she was right. Perhaps a night in their own beds would help them both achieve some clarity.

So why did he feel so crushed, as if Della was already withdrawing from him, despite the fact they still had three nights of their holiday left? He glanced around, hoping to spy her, as if one of her smiles would settle the doubts coiling inside him. Her tepid reaction to his news of a job vacancy had completely swept his feet from under him. He'd assumed she'd be overjoyed to come home, not hesitant. But maybe she was right to apply the brakes. Maybe he should proceed with caution, too. After all, a job in his department represented a significant move for Della, and seeing her every day at work would be an adjustment for them both. Maybe Harvey was too invested in the idea of them working together long-term, whereas Della intended for them to return to the way they were. Maybe he was jumping the gun when he should be preparing himself for the end of their fling instead.

A growing sense of foreboding urged him onwards in his search. If he only knew what she was thinking… He found Della in resus with a patient, a boy around ten years old, and his father. His heart lurched at the sight of her as if they'd been estranged for years, not minutes.

As he approached, Della looked up with no evidence of her earlier doubts. 'Dr Ward, this is Taito. He fell from his trampoline this afternoon. I was just explaining to Dad that he has a fractured femur.'

The boy moaned in pain. Harvey greeted the patient and his father, stepping close to Della to examine the X-ray on the screen, while a trickle of relief calmed his pulse.

'Mid-shaft, spiral fracture,' she said to Harvey, placing a butterfly needle in the crook of Taito's left arm before addressing the boy. 'I'm going to give you some more medicine for the pain.' She injected the painkillers slowly into the vein and then touched the boy's shoulder in comfort, her expression full of her signature compassion.

Harvey's pulse bounded as he watched her work. Della was such a caring person, that big heart of hers making her so hard to resist. No wonder he was struggling.

A fresh wave of panic struck him. He wanted more time.

'Skin traction will help with pain relief,' Harvey said, staring into her eyes, searching for her true feelings, desperate to know how she felt about him to help him understand what was going on inside his own head.

'I'll get that organised with Seema,' she said, holding his eye contact as if silently communicating something he was too confused to see.

'Want me to ring the on-call orthopaedic reg?' he asked, needing to be near her because she made him feel better, but also aware that she was nearing the end of a long day, and he could help out.

'Yes, please,' she said, flicking him a look of gratitude. 'I'll meet you in the office shortly.'

Harvey used the phone in the doctors' office to speak to his orthopaedic colleague, making the referral. Taito's fracture would need internal fixation surgery, but he and Della could pass the case on. He'd not long hung up the phone when Della appeared.

'Long day…' she said, taking the seat beside his to add a note to the patient's file.

'How is Taito?' he asked, wishing he could massage her shoulders, run her bath and pour her a glass of wine. But they'd agreed to spend the night apart.

'He fell asleep as soon as the painkillers kicked in. His poor father felt so guilty.' She turned to face him, her stare full of uncertainty, or perhaps he was just imagining it.

Harvey reached for her hand and wrapped his fingers around hers. 'Why don't you go home, have a relax in the bath, a glass of wine and an early night.'

'Sounds heavenly,' Della said, her stare searching his so he witnessed her doubts. She sighed. Then, without warning, she leaned close and pressed her lips to his, her body sagging against his chest.

'What was that for?' Harvey asked when she pulled back, his hand cupping her face.

'No reason,' she said with a small frown, 'other than I wanted to kiss you. In a few days' time I won't be able to.'

Harvey's pulse thudded harder, the reminder that their time in Fiji would soon be over releasing another cascade of panic. Della leaned in again, slid her fingers through his hair and kissed him slowly and thoroughly as if she was memorising the feel of his lips against hers for when this was over. Harvey gripped her upper arms and kissed her back, more confused than ever but determined to take every scrap of her she would allow in the time they had left.

When they parted, each breathing hard, she

blinked up at him. 'Come home with me,' she whispered. Her eyes were heavy, her pupils dilating.

Excitement energised Harvey's body, mocking his attempts to stay in control of his thoughts and how she made him feel. 'I thought you were tired.' He brushed the hair back from her face.

Suddenly he didn't care about preparing himself for the end of their fling. He wanted as much of Della as he could get until they left the island. Maybe by then, he'd have his conflicted feelings all figured out.

'I am, but I don't care.' She took his hand and dropped her gaze. 'It's just struck me that we only have a few nights left, and I don't want to waste a single second.' She met his stare, hers bold. 'I don't want to have regrets when I leave here.'

Harvey tilted up her chin and brushed her lips with his. 'Neither do I.' He would immerse himself in this relationship until the last minute. Surely by then, a way forward would present itself.

'Let's go,' he said, logging off from the computer. 'I'll run you that bath and pour you a glass of wine.'

'Harvey,' she said, reaching for his arm so he stilled. 'Thanks for thinking of me for the job. I will seriously consider it.'

He nodded, wanting to crush her in his arms and beg her to apply, but maybe Della could see pitfalls he hadn't even considered. 'You're welcome, Della.' Considering her for a colleague was no hardship, given he thought about her every minute of every day. And despite all the reasons for caution, he couldn't see that abating anytime soon.

CHAPTER TWELVE

Two DAYS LATER, jittery with nerves, Harvey walked behind Della, his hands covering her eyes as he guided her into the luxury villa he'd booked for their final night in Fiji.

'Ready?' he asked, sucking in the scent of her freshly washed hair and her light floral perfume, his heart thumping with bittersweet excitement.

Della nodded, her hand gripping his arm. 'You'd better not have brought me to see one of those giant coconut crabs, because that's not funny.'

'Would I do that to you? You hate crabs,' Harvey said, his doubts building because romance wasn't his strong point. 'Now, keep your eyes closed until I say so.' He removed his hands from her eyes and stepped around Della, positioning himself so he could see her reaction. 'Okay, open them.'

Della blinked, quickly glanced his way and then took in the room, which was scattered with flickering tea light candles. The French doors opened to reveal their own private veranda with an in-ground infinity-edged spa pool that overlooked the sea views.

Her eyes widened, and her hands covered her mouth. 'Oh… It's so beautiful. This is so thoughtful of you, Harvey.' She reached for him, her smile worth a hundred words.

Harvey snaked his arm around her waist, drawing her into his arms, relief flooding his system. 'We've had such a busy week, we deserve a treat on our last night. Do you want to have a soak in the spa before we eat?'

'Definitely,' she said, her eyes full of excitement and laughter as she kicked off her sandals and reached for the hem of her dress. Underneath, she wore the pink bikini he loved. While Della climbed in the spa, Harvey hastily tossed aside his shirt, poured two glasses of wine and then joined her.

The water was warm, the sounds of the sea and the Fijian insect life from the surrounding forest soothing background noise. But not even Della's obvious delight could chase off the hollowness deep at the centre of his chest. A huge part of him didn't want to go home. So many times this week, he'd almost raised the subject of them seeing where this relationship could go, and each time, he'd chickened out, kept his mouth shut, his doubts that he could form a committed relationship building. But his head couldn't seem to let the idea go.

'To two weeks in paradise,' Harvey said, making a toast to remind her how far they'd come in such a short time.

Della touched her glass to his, her eyes bright. 'Who'd have thought that being stuck with each other would turn out to be so…rejuvenating.' Before he could comment, she playfully sat astride his lap, resting her arms on his shoulders, leaning in to press a kiss to his lips.

Harvey savoured the contact, his heart thudding wildly. Della seemed to be handling their final night better than him, not that it was a competition. But where he was desperate to talk about the future, to voice his feelings and find out what she was thinking, Della seemed to be intent on keeping things light. It left him wondering if his instincts were way off. That if he tried to talk to her about them, she might dismiss him out of hand.

He swallowed hard as she pulled back, trying not to get lost in her stare. 'So, how do you want to play it?' he asked, his voice strangled with lust and confusion. Before he got too carried away by her touch, her kisses, that seductive look in her eyes, he at least wanted to address Jack's naming day in a fortnight, when they would definitely see each other again.

'Play what?' She shifted on his lap, the position putting her breasts in his line of vision, which was very distracting.

'Us,' he choked out, 'at Jack's naming day, with your family.'

Della tangled her fingers in his hair and tilted his head back, sliding her lips from his earlobe to his jaw, her touch speeding up his already erratic pulse. 'Well, given we agreed to leave *us* behind when we left Fiji, we'll find a way.'

His heart sank further. He closed his eyes, arousal a fire in his blood as she trailed her lips down the side of his neck. But his words, his yearning wanted an outlet before it was too late and they'd succumbed to this endless need for each other. 'But don't you think one of your family—probably Brody, let's be honest—will be able to tell something is different with us?'

It would be a miracle if Harvey managed to keep his eyes off Della when they next met, and if he looked at her, surely someone would be able to see what he was too scared to articulate—how he had feelings for Della he had no idea what to do with. But the two of them exploring more than sex felt ludicrous. An outrageous and risky fantasy. He'd been single by choice for twenty years, and Della… Della was a hearts and flowers romantic who deserved to have her every wish come true. How could a man like him ever be good enough?

What did Harvey know about long-term commitment? What would he have to offer this incredible woman? Even if she did want him, could he step up and be what she needed, or would he ruin everything if he tried, losing people he considered family?

'That's easy.' Della sat back, her expression transparent as she placed her wineglass on the edge of the spa. 'We'll throw Brody off the scent. I'll make a few digs at you, and you can goad me into an argument, perhaps over the wine. No one will ever know.' She chuckled, pressed her lips back to his, and writhed on his lap so he struggled to think of anything beyond how much he wanted her. But beneath the arousal, his stomach knotted.

He didn't want Della and him to revert to the strangers of old, bickering as if these two unexpected and passionate weeks hadn't happened. But Della was obviously happy to leave this, them, behind. Whereas Harvey…? He wasn't sure which way was up, but he was terrified that he'd never be able to switch off this physical craving. He'd found something with her here in Fiji. Nothing as mundane as friendship, more like an intense connection someplace way beyond friends. Mutual acceptance and respect and…obsession. There was no point trying to pretend. He thought about her all the time, wanted to be around her every moment of every day. For the first time in years, he'd developed deep feelings for a woman, a woman who didn't, *couldn't*, feel the same way about him. A woman he needed to protect from the kind of man he'd become, because she deserved so much more than he could give.

The familiar taste of rejection and failure burned his throat, so he held her closer, tighter. 'Do you think we can pull it off?' he asked, placing his wineglass beside hers. 'Not the bickering for Brody's sake, but…you know…the clean break?' His heart raced as if he was a teenager with a crush, asking for a girl's number. He held his breath balanced on the edge of a knife. Harvey had never been less certain of anything in his life or more out of control. But Della did this to him, left him powerless until he wasn't sure whether to run from the feeling or push through it to the brave new world on the other side.

Della stilled, staring down at him with a frown. 'I think we'll be okay. After all, we live in different countries.' She smiled, her fingers moving restlessly through his hair.

Was she making light of their split to protect herself or to let Harvey off the hook? Because they both knew he was in foreign waters here, wanting more than sex. He had no idea what more would even look like for them. He didn't want this fling to end, but nor was he certain he could make her the kind of promises he knew she wanted and deserved after so many years of shutting down his feelings. Was he simply being selfish by trying to hold on? Would he be the ultimate loser if he tried and failed?

'As easy as that, huh?' he asked, barely able to breathe, he was so confused and conflicted. And he hadn't missed the fact that she'd yet to confirm if she was applying for the job in Melbourne.

She frowned, her stare shifting between his eyes. 'It'll be an adjustment. I'll miss this.' Shifting her hips on his lap, she brushed his lips with hers.

Harvey's hands glided from her back to her hips, holding her still. Every move she made, her curves and softness filling his arms were torture to his strung-out body. He wanted to crush her to his chest and pleasure her over and over again until dawn when they needed to leave for the airport. Maybe then, he'd have worked her fully out of his system and everything would make sense. Maybe then, Della would look at him the way she had under the waterfall, as if he, broken, unworthy Harvey, might just be the answer to her dreams. But who was he trying to kid?

'I'll miss this too, Della,' he said, his throat raw with longing. *I'll miss you.* Gripping her waist, he buried his face against her breasts, over the beat of her heart. Now that their last night together was here, he wanted to rewind time. To go back to the start of their two weeks. Or better still, to go back twenty years and be a different man, one who'd overcome his grief and the ingrained belief that there was something unlovable about him and who deserved Della. One who understood that losing Alice, losing his mother's love, had nothing to do with him and everything to do with the unfair randomness of life and the selfish choices of others.

Della was right. He wasn't that powerless kid anymore. Except she made him feel that way, as if one wrong move would shatter the safe, predicable existence he'd clung to most of his adult life. He'd wasted so much time fighting his desire for this woman, when now it was all he could think about.

Della stroked his hair, and he held her tighter. He didn't want their last night to be only about desire. He needed to know Fiji had meant something to her, because it meant something to him.

'Would you have dated me when we first met?' he asked, looking up. 'If I'd been ready to ask you and you'd been single? If I hadn't been grieving and you weren't my best friend's sister?' Regret was pointless. Time travel impossible. But he needed to know that he hadn't been alone in imagining the shadow of what might have been between them all this time.

Della froze, her stare flitting. 'I… I don't know. Perhaps I would… It wasn't that I didn't fancy you, just that we've always wanted different things.'

Harvey nodded, too confused to explain that he wasn't sure what he wanted anymore. Somehow, it was easier to admit how he'd felt about her when they'd first met than how he felt now, tonight. But instinct told him Della was preparing to walk away, and he couldn't blame her. What did he have to offer? Just himself, as lacking as he was?

'I know the timing was wrong for us both, but part of me wishes I'd asked you back then,' he said, his voice thick with emotion. 'Who knows how life might have turned out differently if I had?'

Confused, her frown deepened, her fingers stilling in his hair. 'It's in the past. We can't change it.'

'Right. I guess I wanted you to know that I've always fancied you. I just wasn't ready for a relationship. And even twenty years ago, despite being a bit of a jerk, I was smart enough to know that hurting you would have cost me nearly everything I had—you, Brody, your mum and dad.'

'Harvey...' she whispered, resting her forehead against his, but somehow still seeing right through him. 'You know it wasn't your fault, don't you?'

Harvey froze, his pulse flying. Why hadn't he just seduced her instead of trying to verbalise the storm raging inside him?

'Not your parents' divorce,' she continued, 'or your mother choosing to leave, or Alice's accident.'

'I know.' Those events weren't his fault, but they had shaped him, made him someone who valued emotional control over all else. And look where that had led.

'And you have nothing to prove anymore,' she said, brushing his lips with hers. 'You're in control of your own life.'

The change of subject felt like a goodbye, a pep talk, a final note to see him on his way. Crushed by her emotional withdrawal, Harvey held her tight, pressing his face against her chest. He didn't want her to fix him. He wanted her to want him. To choose him over all men. But he'd seen the same look in her eyes when he'd encouraged her to apply for the Melbourne job. If he pushed for more than this fling, he might discover that he could never be what Della needed, that she wanted so much more than he was capable of. Could he live with that knowledge when he had to live with her in his life?

'Let's go to bed,' she whispered, tilting his head back, her lips finding his, parting, caressing, while her hips rocked on his lap.

Clinging to the distraction of her touch, he gazed up at her. Maybe she was right to remind him this was about pleasure. Maybe this was the only part of her he could have. Maybe once he was away from her, he'd move on as easily as she predicted. Harvey steeled himself against the pleasure her kisses always delivered, his hands cupping her breasts to coax out those moans he loved.

Della gasped, her eyes glazed with arousal as he thumbed her nipples erect. Because he was raw and exposed and ravenous for her, as always, he chased her lips with his. Their tongues met and duelled as their kisses deepened out of control. He might not be able to give her a ring, a family, that white picket fence dream, but he could give her this. Make tonight one she'd always remember.

Harvey slipped his hand between her legs, inside her bikini bottoms, and stroked her. Della broke free of their kiss to stare down at him, her pupils dilating with arousal. Emotions fluttered through her eyes. Arousal, uncertainty, perhaps even fear. But of course she would be scared to expect anything from him, scared to trust that he could be more than a good time, and she was right. The powerless feeling he detested returned. He couldn't let her down. He couldn't lose Della or the other Wiltons from his life. Better to let her go now and keep a part of her forever than to risk losing everything.

Harvey stroked her faster, one arm holding her around her waist. She rode his hand, her eyes on his and her arms braced on his shoulders.

'Kiss me,' he said, because he wanted to forget that this would be the last time he touched her, the last time he held her in his bed and awoke to the scent of her perfume on his pillow.

She whimpered, grasped his neck and lowered her mouth to his. Her hips bucked. He stroked her faster, slid his fingers inside her and braced himself against her wild kisses.

'If you had asked me twenty years ago,' she panted after pulling away, 'I would have said yes.'

Triumph soared in Harvey's chest. He tugged down her bikini top and bent his head, captured her exposed nipple, sucking. She cried out her climax, her slippery body bucking against his under the water. Harvey held her close. Her heart thudded against his cheek where he'd crushed her in his arms. She whimpered and he slid his hand from between her legs, wrapping both arms around her, certain that he should never let her go in case it became the biggest mistake of his life.

Hours later, Della clung to Harvey as the dying cries of her orgasm echoed around the room. The moonlight shone through the window of their bure, streaking the sumptuous bed with surreal shafts of light. She kissed him, snatching breaths between surges of her tongue against his. The entire night, from the moment he'd excitedly collected her and her cases from the staff bungalow at the hospital to when he'd made love to her over and over again, carried a fantastical dreamlike quality. And Della was scared to wake up.

Harvey groaned, tore his mouth from hers and collapsed on top of her, his body racked with the spasms of his climax as he crushed her close, so close she almost lost her breath.

'We have to stop,' Della said, panting, pushing his sweaty hair back from his face. 'We have to stop before we kill each other like those horny mice.' Her plea was feeble, born of exhaustion more than a desire to stop. The night had been both endless and too short. Every time one of them dozed off, the other would reach for them again, their touch, their kisses quickly escalating as if they were both intent on outrunning the passage of time. But it was as if they'd missed their chance twenty years ago, and they both knew it.

Harvey slid from her body and rolled to the side, drawing her onto his chest. He pressed his lips to her head, his arms banded around her shoulders. 'I don't want to stop. I can't seem to.'

Della nodded, her eyelids heavy. 'Me neither.' But as the pleasure subsided, the heavy ache in her chest returned. Her flight to Auckland was leaving in four hours. She could sleep on the plane. If she closed her eyes now, if she fell asleep, their relationship would be over when she awoke, and a part of her never wanted that moment to come.

Harvey's words from earlier scratched at the closed door in her mind. They'd sounded like regrets. But surely Harvey hadn't changed his mind about staying single? He couldn't possibly want a relationship. He didn't do those. Perhaps Della was simply seeing what she wanted to see.

Scared that she was projecting her own feelings onto him, Della closed her eyes. She'd spent all week preparing for this night, their last, holding something back, refusing to rely on her intuition, focussed on the end goal: leaving Fiji and moving on from their fling. Because Harvey might have regrets—everyone did to some extent—but he still wasn't ready to change. Maybe he was too broken to allow himself to be loved. Maybe, because of his mother, he felt inherently unworthy of love. But Della needed to be strong. This time, she couldn't afford to be wrong or settle for a relationship with misaligned expectations. This time, she had to get it right.

'Can I call you from Australia?' he asked, his voice husky with lack of sleep. 'I won't just miss the sex. I'll miss you, too.'

Della's heart fluttered painfully at his words. It had been an intense fortnight. Adjusting to their new reality would feel strange for a while. But could she be Harvey's friend, knowing how close she'd come to falling for him? If they talked, their emotional connection would deepen, at least for Della. Could she then keep her feelings at bay the way she'd tried to every night in his arms this week, or would missing him, craving him, cause those feelings to overwhelm her? Wasn't a clean break the only sure-fire way to protect her heart? After all, she'd tried and failed miserably to wean herself off sleeping with Harvey.

'I don't know, Harvey.' She felt him tense, and her arms reflexively tightened around his chest. 'I'll be honest, I'll struggle to be your friend at the moment.' She felt the thud of his heart under her cheek and went on. 'There's just so much water under the bridge when it comes to us. If we talk, I may weaken next time I see you and end up seducing you again. You know how weak my willpower is.' The dash of humour was intended to soften the blow, but Della had never felt less like smiling, because every word was true and laced with fear.

'Would that be so terrible?' He pressed his lips to the top of her head. 'When we're not bickering, we're very good together.'

Della blinked, her eyes stinging. 'Of course it wouldn't be terrible. But this time here with you has made me realise that maybe I am ready to start dating again. That husband I'm after isn't going to just land in my lap, so I probably need to get out there and find him.'

All Harvey was offering was another night in his bed. As tempting as that was, she'd want so much more. She'd want another night and another and another. Then she'd fall in love with him and want him to be the man of her dreams. Would he ever be ready for that? And could Della afford to put those dreams on hold again and wait around on the off chance that he might change his mind?

He'd told her to be uncompromising when it came to her next relationship, and he was right. If they tried to drag this physical fling out, she'd be forced to one day make the tough choice: amazing sex with Harvey or having it all with someone else. She'd hate herself if she reached her expiration date like all his other women. Because it would be so easy to allow herself to fall in love with the Harvey she'd come to know in Fiji. Maybe they were better off as friends, after all.

'I've had a wonderful time. I'll never forget it.' Gripping his face, she pressed her lips to his, ignoring the flicker of disappointment in his dark stare. She felt it too. It was hard to give up something so good. But Della needed to be selfish, to trust her gut and go after what she wanted, to have it all.

'Me neither,' he said hesitantly.

'And if I get the job in your department, we might end up working together again.' Maybe friends and colleagues were for the best. So why did it suddenly feel like a second-rate consolation prize?

He offered her a smile tinged with sadness she didn't want to acknowledge. 'I'd like that. I really hope you'll apply.'

Della nodded, the burn in her chest, the plummeting of her stomach leaving her to wonder just how she would work with Harvey every day and not want him. Tonight had almost broken her. Their out-of-control need for each other was so profound, she wondered how she would survive the sexual drought to come.

But survive it she must.

CHAPTER THIRTEEN

Two weeks later.

HARVEY SMOOTHED A nervous hand down the front of his polo shirt and yanked open his front door, his heart lurching at the wonderful sight of Della on his doorstep. His pulse galloped so fast he worried he might pass out.

'Della. You look…nice.' *Nice?* Two weeks away from her, pining and picking up the phone to call her, and stalking her social media accounts to see if she was dating anyone, and *nice* was the best he could do?

Before he could reach for her and kiss her, she stepped over the threshold, holding out a bottle of red wine like a shield. 'I brought you a lovely New Zealand Pinot Noir. If you don't like it, you can serve it to Brody. He'll drink anything,' she said, breezing past him without so much as a proper glance.

She headed for the kitchen, where her family were already gathered, leaving Harvey stunned and confused. He closed the door, his stomach in his shoes and his legs threatening to collapse. That wasn't the reunion he'd expected, the reunion he'd played out in his mind on a daily basis. The one where he kissed her, told her that *friends* wasn't working for him, that missing her had made him realise for the first time in twenty years he wanted a real relationship, with *her*, and then kissed her once more. All it had taken to bring about this massive realisation was a bit of physical distance. Without her body asleep next to his, the bed felt too big. Without her smile, her laughter, the challenge in her eyes, beautiful Melbourne seemed drab. Without Della to bounce ideas off, even his work seemed…mundane.

But clearly Della was still set on the charade for her family, acting as if Fiji hadn't happened. And Harvey could understand. He didn't want to answer any questions about them until he'd had a chance to talk to Della alone.

Cursing the wisdom of hosting a barbecue for the Wiltons the night Della had arrived from Auckland, Harvey joined them in his kitchen. He should have met her at the airport, taken her out to dinner instead, kissed her until her eyes glazed with passion and made love to her all night long just to prove that they could never be just friends. That colleagues alone wouldn't work either, because he wanted her more, not less, than when they'd been in Fiji. But what did Della want, and what if it wasn't him?

Thinking back to their reserved farewell kiss in Nadi Airport, just before he'd boarded one plane to Melbourne and Della another to Auckland, Harvey glanced her way. He understood that she'd been protecting herself on that final night when he'd tried to push for more. He was a big risk for someone who wanted lifelong commitment. But was that enough reason for them to completely give up on something so good? If she'd only give him a chance, he'd show her that his feelings were genuine. That he was ready to let her in and try to be what she needed.

Brody kissed his sister on the cheek, refusing to take the bottle of wine Harvey set in front of him. 'Not for me. I'm a changed man.' He cast a nervous glance at his wife, who was conspicuously sipping a soft drink. 'Now that Dells is here,' Brody continued, 'we may as well tell you all—Amy is pregnant again. Jack's having a little sister!'

Jenny Wilton hugged her daughter-in-law, and Brody's dad, Graham, shifted Jack in his arms to embrace his son. Congratulations flew. But while Harvey was happy for his friend, his eyes were glued to Della's reaction.

She stood frozen, her eyes blinking rapidly as

if she was fighting tears. Harvey's heart jolted in his chest. He'd never seen Della cry. His arms ached to hold her, to whisper how much he'd missed her these endless two weeks, to kiss her and make her a hundred promises that might put a smile back on her face. But what if his promises weren't enough? What if she stonewalled him again like she had in Fiji?

'I'm so happy for you,' she said bravely, snapping out of her trance to hug Amy and then Brody.

'It's early days,' Amy said, laughing, 'and we don't know if it's a sister or brother yet, but Brody seems to think he's telepathic.'

To give himself something to do beyond clearing the house of the other Wiltons so he could be alone with Della, Harvey collected a bottle of fizz from the fridge and popped the cork. 'Just a drop to celebrate,' he said, handing a grinning Brody a glass.

Harvey offered Della a glass of champagne, trying to catch her eye, but she was avoiding looking at him. Instead she declined, putting her arm around Amy's waist. 'I'll abstain in solidarity with Amy, seeing as Brody has no willpower.'

The excited chatter continued as the Wiltons drifted outside to the deck. Why wouldn't she look at him? Yes, they'd agreed to a clean break—

he'd done what she asked and not called—agreed to act normal in front of Della's family. The last thing they needed were intrusive questions when their relationship was so…fragile. But how could she act as if that fortnight in Fiji had never happened, when a huge part of Harvey wanted to announce to the world that he wanted her in his life? Not as a friend or a colleague, but as a partner.

Harvey's stomach twisted with doubt. Maybe Della wasn't as sure about him as he was about her. Maybe she wanted more than she believed he could offer. Maybe if he pushed her again, he might ruin what they already had and lose her from his life. That wasn't an option.

'So, what did Harvey get up to in Fiji, sis?' Brody asked, flicking Harvey a knowing look. 'Any wild nights to report? Did he leave a trail of broken hearts scattered all over the islands?'

'Don't ask me,' Della snapped, avoiding Harvey's stare. 'Ask him. He's *your* friend.'

It was the kind of thing she might have said before Fiji, before they'd become lovers, before he'd opened up to her about his mother in a way he'd never done with anyone else. It was part of the act they'd agreed to, so why did Harvey feel as if she'd physically punched him in the gut?

'Oh, I have asked him,' Brody said playfully, completely missing the tension between Harvey and Della, 'but he's been uncharacteristically tight-lipped. There must have been someone, though. He hasn't had so much as a coffee date since he's been back. If I didn't know better, I'd say he'd met someone he actually cared about.'

Harvey's entire body tensed as he willed Della to look his way. He *had* met someone he cared about—*her*. He wanted her to want him, to fight for him, not disown him. He wanted to matter to her enough that she chose him, here and now in front of her family, people he also considered *his* family. But what if her apparent coldness wasn't an act? What if she'd easily reverted to her feelings of contempt now that their fling was done? What if everything he'd confided in her, everything they'd shared, meant nothing?

Feeling nauseous, Harvey shot Brody a warning a look. Normally he wouldn't care about being the butt of his friend's joke. But something seemed off with Della. Perhaps she was upset about her brother's announcement.

'Oh, I doubt it,' Della said, finally glancing Harvey's way. 'You know what they say—a leopard never changes its spots.' Her expression was another physical blow—confusion, anguish, a flicker of longing gone before Harvey could be certain of it. She turned back to Brody. 'But I was there to work, not to catalogue your friend's female cast-offs.' Spinning on her heel, she joined her parents, who were sitting with

Jack on the grass. On seeing his aunt, Jack held out his chubby fists. Della swung him up into her arms, her face beaming with the first genuine smile of the evening.

Harvey's entire body sagged, his pulse thrumming with hunger. He wanted Della to look at *him* that way. He didn't want to play it cool. He didn't care about awkward questions. He'd rather announce to her family that he wanted her to move back to Melbourne so they could try and have a proper relationship.

Hearing how absurd and inadequate his solution sounded in his head, Harvey deflated. How could Della and he, of all men, work out when she was already way ahead of him, looking for love, a husband, a family of her own? She'd rejected his attempts to start a conversation about them back in Fiji, as good as telling him he wasn't relationship material. He wasn't good enough for her. Felling utterly powerless, he glanced at Brody and winced.

'What on Earth did you do this time to upset Della?' Brody asked sheepishly, as if at last he was finally picking up on the tension between them, the weird dynamic that didn't quite ring true.

Harvey shrugged, his chest hollow, all the excitement of seeing Della again draining away. 'Just existed, I think, mate. Same as usual.'

Only there was one additional thing that wasn't usual—the way he felt inside, as if he'd explode unless he could convince Della to hear him out. With a sickening lurch of his stomach, Harvey realised he might already be falling in love with Della, and it wasn't going to be anywhere near enough.

Della stacked the final plate into the dishwasher, her head all over the place and heart aching. Outside, happy conversations and laughter of her family swirled around. Tomorrow, Jack's naming day would be a joyous occasion, but her smiles felt insincere, and she could barely look at Harvey, so strong was the desire to hurl herself into his arms and make him want her forever.

Della swallowed down the sense of panic. The past two weeks without him had been a living hell. She'd been wrong; the physical distance, the lack of contact, the clean break…*nothing* had helped her get over their fling. *Nothing* was back to normal. Her feelings, the ones she'd tried to deny and sweep under the rug in Fiji, were bigger than ever, especially now that she'd seen Harvey again. The hurt in his eyes when she'd tried to throw Brody off the scent had crushed her.

With a trembling hand, she closed the dishwasher and went in search of Harvey's bathroom. She needed a moment to herself in case she broke down in front of both Harvey and her family and told them exactly what had happened in Fiji. She'd almost spluttered when Brody had asked about wild nights, because there had been plenty of those. As for broken hearts, she'd na-ively assumed hers was untouchable, but Harvey had found a way to get under her guard, to make her fall for him, until she'd become the cliché she'd mocked other women for: past her expira-tion date, but left wanting more. So much more.

She'd stupidly fallen in love with Harvey, a man who couldn't love her back because he'd spent years shutting down his emotions and feeling unworthy of love. And that wasn't all. That morning, before leaving Auckland for Mel-bourne, she'd taken a pregnancy test, discover-ing she was pregnant.

Locking herself in the bathroom now, Della rested her hand on her stomach, choked with happiness. She was finally achieving one of her dreams. A baby. Harvey's baby. But it changed nothing. Of course she needed to tell him, and soon. How would he take the news? Would he be angry? Feel trapped? She had no doubt that he cared for Della and that, in time, he'd do right by their child. But that wasn't how she'd envi-sioned having a family. She wanted to be in love and loved in return. She wanted to build a home with that love of her life. She wanted forever.

Della blinked away the sting in her eyes. Harvey had urged her to be uncompromising when it came to her dreams and desires, to reach for it all and never settle. Of course he couldn't have known that he'd become tangled up in those dreams. That she'd want to spend the rest of her life with *him*, have *his* baby. But Della couldn't make him feel something for her that he just wasn't capable of. Better to take what was on offer, his friendship and respect. Better for them to focus on being parents, separate but united for their child. This time, it was better to strategically settle than to risk losing a chunk of her heart she wasn't sure she'd survive without.

While she washed her hands, she splashed cold water on her face and avoided looking at her reflection in the mirror. She knew what she'd see. A woman in love. A woman who in fact, despite all her tough talk and Harvey's encouragement, *couldn't* have it all. A woman who'd made another mistake and fallen for a broken man incapable of loving her back. Because to Harvey, love was weakness. Powerlessness. A price too high.

Della emerged from the bathroom, reluctant to head back outside just yet. Distracted by the framed photographs lining the hallway, she took a closer look. She'd never really noticed them before, but they were pictures of Harvey with all the important people in his life. One of him and Brody in their twenties, dressed in tuxedos at some medic's ball. One of Harvey and Bill dressed in hiking gear on the top of Victoria's Mount Oberon. One of Christmas at the Wiltons', everyone wearing paper hats as they raised a toast to the camera.

Her family was Harvey's too. He loved them and they him. All the more reason for Della to tread with caution so neither of them lost what they valued. She spied herself in the last photo, struggling to identify which Christmas it was. But even then, all those years ago, some part of her had wanted Harvey, had been halfway in love with him. She would likely always have unresolved feelings for Harvey. But she'd survive that. What she wouldn't survive was loving him with her whole heart when he didn't love her back.

Della was just about to turn away, to head to the garden and tell her family she was calling it a night, when a pair of hands gripped her waist. 'There you are. I've been trying to get you alone all night.'

His warm breath tickled the side of her neck and she shuddered, his touch sparking her body alive as if she'd been in a coma for two long weeks. Della turned, bracing herself against how handsome he was, how it physically hurt to look at him because he could never be hers. His eyes danced with the excitement she'd waited two endless weeks to see.

'Come with me,' he said. She meekly followed, clinging to his hand as he tugged her into a nearby room, which turned out to be his home office.

He shut the door and pulled her into his arms. The force of wanting him almost buckled her knees, but panic beat at her ribs.

'Shouldn't we head back outside before they come looking for us?' she said feebly as he cupped her face and slid his fingers into her hair, tilting up her chin.

'Brody's taken Amy and Jack home,' he breathed against her lips. 'I think both your parents have dozed off sitting around the fire pit.' Without another word, he pressed his lips to hers and just let them sit there for a handful of seconds as he breathed in deeply. Della sighed, sagged against him, her entire body melting as if she was finally home. But he couldn't be her safe place. She needed to be strong for their baby and for her own stupid heart.

'God, I've missed you,' he said, pulling back to stare deep into her eyes.

Della saw longing and desire and euphoria in the depths of his eyes, but it still wasn't enough. She wanted more of him. She wanted all of him—the good and the bad and the broken. She wanted impossible things.

'Why didn't you tell me when you were arriving?' he said, wrapping his arms around her shoulders so her head rested on his chest. 'I'd have picked you up from the airport.'

Della shrugged, her heart so sore she could barely breathe. 'You were busy here, and how would we have explained that to the others?'

Harvey stiffened, rested his hands on her shoulders and peeled her away so he could look at her. 'Is everything okay? You've been avoiding me all night. I've been going out of my mind. I wanted to kiss you so badly.'

'I thought the plan was to play it cool,' Della lied. She'd ignored him because to be close to him was torture. Because she'd almost snapped so many times tonight and confessed that she loved him. Because the part of her that yet again had realised too late she'd have to compromise her dreams wanted him anyway, as she'd known she would.

Della swallowed, stepping back but wishing she was still in his arms, where things made a twisted kind of sense. 'We don't need Brody and his intrusive questions. I swear Amy is a saint for putting up with my brother.'

'Can you stay?' he asked, reaching for her again. 'Here. With me, tonight? After everyone else leaves.'

Della rested her hand on his chest, felt the rapid pound of his heart, wished that it beat with love for her. 'I can't… We agreed.' Her throat ached with longing. Why had she ever thought she could be this man's friend? She'd known it had been impossible the first time she'd met him. Now, twenty years later, when she knew him better than ever, there was no hope. She loved him. She craved him. She wanted him. *Friends* was for the runner-up.

'Della… I've been thinking,' he said when she stayed silent, because she was desperately trying not to cry. 'I've missed you so badly since I arrived home.'

'Me too,' she said, her throat tight. She refused to cry. She didn't want to blurt out her irrelevant feelings or her news about the baby. She'd planned it all on the flight. She'd tell him tomorrow, after Jack's naming day party.

He smiled, and her heart cracked a little more. 'I really want you to apply for the job in my department. Us working together has to be better than this—missing each other, waking up alone, not to mention the abstinence.' He shot her a playful smile that two weeks ago she could have returned. But not now.

'I... I'm not sure, Harvey.' Della shook her head, looked down. She wanted more than sex. She wanted it all. She always had. The only change was that she wanted it with him—Harvey Ward.

'I know it's complicated,' Harvey rushed on, 'and I don't have the first clue what I'm doing, but if you move back here, maybe we could, you know, try dating. Each other, I mean.' He exhaled a sigh, as if speaking those words had left him exhausted.

Della's chest ached. Of course he would struggle with dating, but she could see how hard he was trying. That he genuinely meant what he'd said. That the first tentative step towards a relationship was a huge step for Harvey. But they'd always been too different when it came to commitment, and that hadn't changed. Della was miles ahead, a place where she was sure to get hurt. And what then? What about the baby?

'You know I haven't done this in a very long time,' he continued, misinterpreting her hesitance. 'I know I'm a risk, but it could work. *We* could work.' Before she could reply, he hauled her close, bringing her lips up to his, sliding his tongue against hers, filling her body with love hormones. Della surrendered, luxuriating in his kisses, which, after two parched weeks in the desert, felt like heaven. But the high faltered, her head intruding. She'd have to turn him down. She'd have to tell him why.

Because she was too scared to part with her secret just yet, because she wanted him, one last time, in spite of how ridiculously out of sync they were when it came to relationships, Della allowed herself the indulgence of his strong arms, his frantic kisses, the hot possessive surge of his tongue against hers. Oh, how she'd missed him, the breadth of his smile and the playful glint in his eyes. The feel of his strong arms and the beat of his heart. The way he believed in her and the way he made her feel. She panted, preparing to stop this. To walk away before any more of her heart was eroded, but her fingers flexed in his shirt, her head falling back so he could ravage her neck, her moans encouraging.

'That was the worst two weeks of my life,' he said, hoisting her onto the desk. One of his thighs slotted between her legs as he pressed kisses over her face, her neck, the tops of her breasts and back to her lips. 'Every day I wanted to call you. The only reason I didn't call was to give you the space you wanted, to pretend that we could be friends. But it's not working for me.'

As his lips parted hers once more, his hand cupped her breast through her dress. Pregnancy hormones had made her sensitive, but his touch set her alight, inflamed her from head to toe.

She twisted his hair in her fingers and rubbed the hard length of him through his shorts. Just one more time… Then, at the end of the weekend, she'd tell him about the baby and fly back to Auckland, where she could patch up her bruised heart away from this temptation.

Reaching for his fly, she dragged her kiss-swollen lips from his. 'Hurry,' she said, 'I want you.' If this was the only part of him she could have, she'd take it and worry about the price later.

Harvey didn't argue. While she undid his shorts and pushed them over his hips, taking him in her hand, he lifted her dress and shoved her underwear down her legs, his tongue in her mouth.

Della spread her thighs, making room for his hips, casting the closed office door a nervous glance. But she was too far gone to care about interruptions, too high on the decadence of Harvey's touch to voice caution. Too lovesick to protect her battle-worn heart. She would love him with her body, silently say goodbye. Then she'd walk away from one dream and focus on being the best parent she could be.

Dragging his mouth from hers, Harvey dropped to his knees, shoving her dress up her thighs. 'I locked the door,' he said before covering her with his mouth.

Della closed her eyes against the intense wave of pleasure. Dizzy with it, she braced one hand on the desk behind her and tunnelled the other into Harvey's hair, holding on for dear life.

'Harvey,' she gasped, looking down at him. His eyes were dark with desire and determination, his hands on her thighs, gripping her tight. Pleasure built and built, the sharp ache only a fraction of the pain she'd endured these two weeks without him. But she couldn't keep him. She had to put the baby first. Put herself first.

Her moans grew. She released Harvey's hair and covered her mouth, bit the back of her hand to hold them inside. As if he knew her body, knew how close she was, Harvey jerked to his feet, gripped her hips and slowly pushed inside her. Della clung to his shoulders, wrapped her legs around his hips and dragged his mouth down to hers. Harvey bucked into her, his pace as frantic as the beat of her heart, his kisses as deep as his possession of her body, his passion for her almost enough to make her change her mind. Almost.

Della wanted more than passion. More than really great sex. She wanted him to love her as desperately as she loved him. She wanted them to raise their baby together in that house with the clichéd white picket fence. She wanted him to feel the terrifying fear and powerlessness of love and want it anyway, with *her*. But those dreams belonged to Della, not to Harvey.

Her orgasm ripped through her, and she sobbed his name. Harvey crushed her in his arms and groaned, joining her, his fingers and his whispers in her hair.

'I missed you,' he said, his breath see-sawing in his chest. 'I missed you so much.'

Della hid her face against his neck, blinking the sting of tears from her eyes. That had been a big mistake. 'I'd better go before my parents come looking for one of us.' She pushed him away, slid from the desk and scooped up her underwear from the floor. She needed to get away from him before she begged him to love her.

'You're leaving?' he said, confusion clouding his handsome face as he tucked himself back into his shorts. 'Just hang around until they leave. Stay the night. I'll make you breakfast, and we can go to Jack's thing together.'

'I can't, Harvey. I—' she broke off, realisation dawning. She couldn't wait any longer. She had to tell him now. He deserved to know about the baby, and her confession, the knowledge that he was going to be a father, would put everything back into perspective for him the way it had for Della that morning. She wanted him like oxygen, but this was no longer just about her desires.

'Did you see the job's been advertised?' he

pressed, a desperate look in his eyes. 'You should apply. They need someone to start as soon as possible.'

'Harvey, we need to talk.' She straightened her dress and folded her arms across her waist, holding her fractured pieces together.

'Okay, come and have a drink. Perhaps your parents have already left.'

Della shook her head. 'No. I don't want a drink. I just want you to listen.' Just like they had when they'd left Fiji, it was better to make a clean break of it now. The sex was over, as great as it had been. Now there were bigger issues to work on than if they should be colleagues or whether or not they could make a relationship work.

'Okay. I'm listening.' He reached for her hand, and she paced away. If he touched her again, she'd mess this up, say the wrong things, beg him to love her or worse, settle for only a part of him, not the whole.

'I didn't want to tell you until tomorrow, after the party,' she began, a chill spreading along her bare arms, 'but I'm pregnant, Harvey.' She looked up, saw the flash of disbelief in his eyes and rushed on. 'We made a baby in Fiji. Probably that time in the waterfall.'

Confusion shifted in his stare. He opened his mouth to speak. Closed it again. Shook his head, as dumbfounded as she'd been that morning, seeing those two pink lines.

'I know I reassured you that I was on the pill,' she rushed on, 'which I was. But obviously I must have missed one or something. And I know that you never wanted kids. I know this—' she placed her hand on her stomach '—is my dream, not yours. But I want you to know that you don't have to feel responsible. You don't have to do anything or say anything or be anything you're not ready to be. I understand.'

Poor Harvey. He'd only just decided that he might want a relationship, and now he was going to be a father. Talk about life in fast forward… At his bewilderment, she winced, hating herself for her lack of willpower. If she hadn't slept with him again, maybe she could have kept her secret until a more appropriate time. 'I know it's a lot to take in. You're probably angry and upset—'

'I'm not angry,' he said, his jaw clenched as he scrubbed a hand through his hair, glancing down at her flat stomach. 'Are you…okay?'

Della nodded, brushing aside his concern. If he carried on being wonderful and thoughtful, she was going to cry. As it was, this baby would probably be born holding a box of tissues, she'd cried so much over Harvey this past fortnight.

'Obviously this weekend is about Amy and Brody and baby Jack,' she said, also reminding herself that she couldn't be properly excited yet and tell anyone else. 'I know we'll need to explain about us eventually, but I think it's best if we keep this to ourselves for now and figure everything else out later. I'll, um…call you from Auckland, and we can talk everything through.'

Harvey's frown deepened, his helpless expression hardening. 'Wait,' he said, stepping forward and reaching for her arm.

Della stepped back, ducked out of his reach. She couldn't let him touch her again or she'd break down.

'You're going back to Auckland?' he asked, incredulous, his stare carrying pain and accusation.

Nausea swirled in her stomach. 'Of course, Harvey. I live there. My home is there. My job.' She couldn't just drop everything. She needed time to think.

'So you're not going to apply for the job here?' He gripped the back of his neck and paced back and forth. 'Where we could raise our baby together?'

A wild flutter of hope bloomed in her chest. Could she do that? Move home, work with Harvey, have his baby and hope that in time, he might fall in love with her? Could she settle for so little when she wanted it all? If it worked, it would be everything she'd ever dreamed. But if it failed, would she survive? Maybe if she hadn't fallen in love with him, she could return and just see what happened. But it was too late for what-ifs.

'I'm not sure yet,' she whispered, fear and guilt and loathing forcing her stare from his. 'I'll certainly think about the job. But like you, I'm in shock. I only found out about the baby myself this morning, and now I have to think about things like maternity leave...' Della swallowed hard, wishing dreams were that easy. She knew from experience that reaching for it all, pinning her hopes on a man who wasn't sure what he wanted, could backfire. She couldn't make that mistake again, not when there was their baby to consider. She needed to trust her instincts.

He came to a standstill and stared her way. 'So, if you're not sure about the job, you're even less sure about me, about us having a relationship? And yet you let me prattle on about dating, knowing you were going to turn me down.'

Della pressed her lips together, her throat raw with emotion. 'I'm sorry. I wasn't thinking straight.' Had she selfishly used him again? 'I just know that I need to put the baby first. *We* need to put the baby first. This isn't about us anymore, and you and I still want different things.' Dating wasn't enough, not when she loved him so desperately. She'd overreached before, pushed for more and lost. It was better to forget about love and focus on the baby.

'I get it.' Harvey nodded, his stare bleak. 'I'm fine as a sperm donor, I'm fine for sex, but I'm just not up to scratch when it comes to relationships.'

'I didn't say that,' she said, looking away from the pain in his eyes. 'I want us to do this, the baby, together. I just haven't figured out all the details yet.'

'It's okay. I understand,' Harvey said, heading for the door. 'You'll have my baby, but good old Harvey couldn't possibly be anything serious, least of all a husband, right, not when there's probably a better option out there somewhere?'

He left the room, left Della with the echo of his pain and resentment. Rather than face her parents, rather than hurt herself or Harvey any more tonight, Della slipped out of the front door and escaped.

CHAPTER FOURTEEN

HARVEY PRESSED HIS lips to the top of Jack's head and breathed in his clean baby smell, his stare glued to the door of the party venue for a first glimpse of Della. He'd arrived early at the trendy restaurant near Brody and Amy's suburb, which had a small function room for events. His house was too big and too quiet now that he knew not only that he was going to be a father, but that Della wanted nothing more to do with him beyond some depressing shared custody arrangement.

She'd rejected him, as much as told him he wasn't good enough for her to risk her heart, that she could never love a man like him. And he couldn't even be angry, because maybe she was right.

'Are you nervous?' Brody asked, reaching for his son.

Nervous? He was bereft. Della might as well have ripped his heart out of his chest last night and looked down on it with disappointment. He wasn't enough for her, even after everything they'd shared, even when he'd offered to give her everything he could, even when they'd made a child together.

'I'm not nervous,' he reassured Brody, chilled to the bone, because he was so gutted by her rejection he couldn't even be properly excited by the news of his baby. 'I'll be fine.' If *fine* meant desolate, inadequate, helpless like never before.

'The others are risking being late,' Brody said about Della and Mr and Mrs W, looking slightly harassed. He bounced on the balls of his feet to keep the baby happy.

'Should I call Della?' Harvey asked, tension tightening his shoulders. 'Find out where they are?' Maybe they were having car trouble. Maybe Della was ill or there was something wrong with the baby. He'd give her two more minutes, and then he was going to look for her.

Brody scoffed, handing the baby his phone to stop him fussing. 'You calling her would only make her grumpy. We don't want bickering today of all days.'

Harvey rubbed a hand down his face in frustration. Was his friend truly that blind? Why had he never noticed the way Harvey felt about Della? The way he'd *always* felt? Was Harvey that good at hiding his feelings? Because now, when it was over between them, when he'd finally realised that he'd fallen deeply in love with Della in Fiji, he could finally admit that those feelings had always run deep inside him, waiting for the timing to be right. Except nothing was right without Della.

'Haven't you ever stopped to wonder why Della and I are always at each other's throats?' he snapped, taking his frustration out on his clueless friend.

Brody shrugged, distracted. 'You're just too different, that's all.'

'That's not all.' He couldn't do it any longer, pretend that he wasn't crazy about her, that he just wanted sex or friendship or some depressing co-parenting situation. He wanted Della. 'This might be hard for you hear,' he said, past the point of no return, 'but I've always fancied your sister.'

Brody looked up, startled.

'When I first met her,' Harvey continued, 'I was in such a bad place, I knew I couldn't act on it without hurting her or messing up our friendship.'

'My sister?' Brody gaped in disbelief.

Harvey nodded and gripped the back of his neck, his panic mounting. 'I'm in love with her,' he said in a rush. '*She's* the one I care about. *She's* the reason everything has changed for me.' *She* was worth this sickening feeling of fear and inadequacy that made him feel eight years old again.

Brody's eyebrows shot up, and then a slow grin spread over his face. 'Harvey Ward finally falling in love, and it's for my little sister?'

Harvey shook his head and paced away in disgust. 'I shouldn't have told you,' he muttered foully. This was serious. He loved her and he'd lost her because she couldn't believe in him, couldn't want him, couldn't choose him.

'Don't be like that,' Brody said, sobering. 'Does she love you too?'

Harvey shot his friend an incredulous look. 'Don't be stupid. She's an intelligent woman. She could never take me seriously, and she's probably right not to. I don't know the first thing about committed relationships. And I don't want to let her down or hurt her. She's been through enough.' Della was scared, too. Scared to trust her instincts, scared to be hurt again, scared to want her dreams. Why would she take a chance on a beginner like him, especially now that they had their baby to consider? But he'd keep that part of the story to himself for now.

'That bickering you two always do, you know that's two-sided, right?' Brody said, as if he'd completely missed the point Harvey was trying to make.

'Yeah, so?' Harvey checked the time, frantic

now for Della to arrive so he could ensure she was okay.

'Duh…' Brody said, as if reverting to a teenager. 'Della's always had a bit of thing for you. I used to tease her about it. I never told you, obviously, because…you know…she's my sister.'

Harvey shook his head, in no way comforted. Just because she'd always fancied him, just because they were great together physically, didn't mean she was ready to trust him, of all men, with her massive heart. She wasn't even ready to be his colleague, to raise their baby with him, to give him a chance to forge a proper relationship. She didn't want him, and there was nothing he could do to change that.

'It doesn't matter,' Harvey said, too heartsore to explain the details. 'She wants us to be friends.' To raise their baby together but nothing more.

Brody frowned, sceptically, realisation seeming to dawn. 'You haven't told her, have you? That you're in love with her.'

Harvey winced, his chest too small for his lungs. 'I tried…last night…' But he hadn't been able to get the words out. A part of him, the part that had shut down any emotional connection for the past twenty years, still worried he was unworthy of love, especially the love of a woman as amazing as Della.

'Seriously?' Brody asked, inching closer and lowering his voice. 'Don't try, just tell her.'

Harvey curled his hands into fists. Would she care when she'd already decided a relationship with him wasn't enough? Was he setting himself up for another slap of rejection if he told her his true feelings? Was he at risk of not just losing Della, but also of their chance to be parents who got along and respected each other?

'Don't be stupid, man,' Brody pressed. 'She's flying back to Auckland tonight. If you don't tell her today, you might regret it.'

Harvey nodded numbly, his brain firing normally for the first time this weekend. Of course he would regret it. He loved Della, and she needed to know. Even if she could never take him seriously or love him back, he should tell her how she'd made him believe in love again.

'I'm going to find her,' he said, heading for the exit without waiting for permission.

'Don't be late,' Brody called after him. 'My son is counting on you.'

Graham Wilton pulled into the last available parking space outside the restaurant where Jack's naming day party was taking place and turned off the engine.

Della's stomach lurched with despair and anguish. How would she face Harvey today and not completely break down? She'd hurt him last night. Thrown his offer of dating back in his face. Rejected him, just like his mother.

'Can you give us a moment, darling?' Della's mother said to her husband from the passenger seat. 'I just need a word with Della.'

Della shifted in the back seat of the car, checking her watch. 'We're cutting it pretty fine, Mum.' The last thing she needed when she was feeling so bereft was her mum digging around in Della's head.

'This won't take long,' Jenny said, popping her seat belt and turning to face her daughter. 'Especially if you just come out and tell me what's wrong instead of denying it.'

Della sighed, glancing down at her hands twisting in her lap. Of course her mother would pick up on her mood. 'Nothing's wrong,' she started, scared that if she began the story, she'd cry and ruin Jack's photos with her blotchy red face. She looked up, met her mother's sympathetic stare. 'I'm pregnant, that's all.'

Jenny's hand gripped Della's. 'That's wonderful news. I'm so happy for you. Are you feeling okay?'

Della nodded robotically. 'I'm fine. It's very early. Obviously it's Jack's day, and I don't want to tell anyone else yet.'

Jenny nodded, her astute expression turning curious. 'Who's the father?'

Della dragged in a deep breath. This was the tricky part. The risk of breaking down and confessing to her mother that she'd stupidly fallen in love with Harvey Ward. 'It's Harvey.'

Her mother's eyes widened. 'Our Harvey?'

'Of course, Mum. I don't know any other Harveys.' Now that she'd told him her news, now that she'd protected her heart and put the baby first, now that she'd relied on her instincts and refused to settle for less than she deserved, she was supposed to feel better. But if anything, she felt worse. She'd barely slept a wink last night, replaying that last conversation over and over until nothing made sense. Reliving the hurt in Harvey's eyes. The rejection and the heartbreaking acceptance, as if he'd been expecting it all along.

'Oh, my...' Jenny said, with a flash of respect. 'I didn't know you two were—'

'We're not,' Della said flatly. 'It happened in Fiji.'

Jenny nodded, knowingly. 'Of course. Well, he's always liked you.'

Della looked up, her heart withering a little more. If only he could do more than like her. If only he wanted more than a *try it and see* relationship. If only he could love her. 'Yes, well, I just want to get through today, so if you could not mention it to Dad or Brody or Amy, and maybe stop looking at me like that.'

'Like what?' Jenny asked innocently. 'Like I'm about to ask what your plans are?'

'Exactly.' Della sighed as Jenny waited for her to elaborate. 'My plan is to go back to New Zealand and have a good long think,' she said, caving to pressure. 'My plan is to focus on raising my baby, with as much input from Harvey as he wants, obviously.'

'And what about you and Harvey?' Jenny asked, a flicker of sympathy in her eyes. 'What about having a relationship?'

'Come on, Mum. This is Harvey,' Della said, glancing out of the car window to stop herself from crying. 'He's not really ready for a relationship, not that I can blame him. But the most important thing for all of us, him, me and the baby, is if we're…friends.'

Jenny frowned, her eyes full of questions. 'But you're in love with him.'

'I am.' The admission should have filled her with joy.

'How is that going to factor into your *friendship*?'

Della ducked her head in shame. 'Obviously it's not. I'll get over it. I'll put the baby first, and I'll be fine.'

Jenny nodded in agreement. 'Yes, you will. But you won't have everything you've ever wanted. Does Harvey know that you're in love with him? Have you told him how you feel? Because if you really love him, it's not just going to go away, and he deserves to know something so important.'

Della shook her head, her eyes burning. 'No. I… I didn't think it was relevant. We still want different things.'

Except what had Harvey meant when he'd said 'good old Harvey couldn't possibly be anything serious, least of all a husband'?

'Harvey thinks he wants to try and have a relationship,' she went on, more confused than ever, 'but I can't be his trial run, putting my feelings on hold, loving him but waiting around to see if a relationship is what he genuinely wants. I just can't.' It would destroy her.

'But if you haven't told him how you feel and what *you* want, you haven't really given him a chance to step up, have you?' Jenny tilted her head, seeing way too much for Della's liking. 'What if he needs to know that you love him? What if he loves you too?'

Della glared, her heart in her throat. Of course, Harvey needed to be loved as much as the next person, perhaps more so after everything he'd been through. She shook her head even as hope rushed through her like an electrical storm. 'He can't love me. He's spent most of his adult life shutting down, keeping people out.'

Jenny smiled sadly. 'And you're still scared to want it all in case you make another mistake.'

Della swallowed, sick to her stomach. Had she written Harvey off too soon, because she was still scared to trust her judgement, still settling for less than she deserved? Still terrified to reach for all of her dreams? Had she unfairly judged him, rejected him the way his mother had, when in reality, she loved and wanted every inch of him, even if he didn't love her back?

'You've always been scared to fail,' Jenny said, squeezing Della's fingers. 'I blame myself and your father. We inadvertently created a very competitive household. But your drive is your strength. Don't let one relationship failure hold you back from having everything you want. Tell Harvey how you feel and give him a chance.'

Della nodded numbly, feeling stupid. A small, building sense of panic was choking her. Her mother was right.

'Come on,' Jenny said, opening the passenger side door. 'We'd better go inside. The ceremony is about to start.'

Della slammed the car door and rushed inside the venue. Was she too late to undo the damage she'd inflicted last night when she'd hurt both

Harvey and herself with her fear? Her mother was right. Harvey deserved to know that she loved him, even if he couldn't return her feelings. To know that, of all men, Della chose *him*.

CHAPTER FIFTEEN

HARVEY HADN'T MADE it to Della in time. Just as she and her mother had walked into the room, her eyes meeting his for an electrifying beat, the celebrant had announced it was time to start. All throughout the naming day ceremony, as together they'd promised to guide and support Jack, he'd struggled to take his eyes off her. She looked beautiful, her simple blue dress matching the colour of her eyes, and her hair casually pinned up to expose her neck. It had been torture fighting the urge to drag her aside and tell her how he felt about her, but somehow he'd managed to put Brody, Amy and Jack first temporarily.

Outside in the garden at the side of the restaurant, Harvey's cheek muscles twitched from the pressure of maintaining a semi-fake smile. But he didn't want to ruin Jack's photos.

'And one last smile, please,' the photographer said, snapping the final photo—Amy and Brody in the centre holding Jack with Harvey and Della at either end.

The minute the photographer checked the shot in the digital display, Harvey moved to intercept Della, panic like ice in his veins. But his patience had run out.

'Della, we need to talk,' he said as Amy and Brody wandered back inside with Jack.

'Yes, of course, we do,' she said, blinking up at him. 'Harvey, I'm so sorry about last night.' She reached for his arm. 'I was all over the place. I'd like to blame my hormones, but I think that would be a lie.'

Harvey shook his head, cutting her off, drawing her deeper into the shade of a tree out of the sun. 'No. *I'm* sorry.' He took her hand from his arm and squeezed her fingers. 'I was stupid, Della. I was so excited to see you after these past two weeks that I stepped in my own way, and I forgot to tell you the most important thing.'

He gripped her arms, wishing they were somewhere more romantic than a garden so he could convince her that he meant what he was about to say. But he'd just have to risk that this, here and now, would be enough. 'I love you, Della. I fell in love with you in Fiji, and I should have told you as soon as I realised.'

She blinked, her eyes wide with confusion and doubt.

'I was scared,' he rushed on, his hands skimming her upper arms, because he couldn't not touch her. 'Scared that I'm not enough for you, because I'm a forty-two-year-old man who's never been in love before, not like this.' He pressed a fist to the centre of his chest, where it burned the most. 'Scared that you deserve someone better at relationships. That if I tried to be what you need, I'd fail and let you down, and I never want to be a man who lets you down.' He shook his head, the idea abhorrent.

'Harvey...' she whispered, her eyes shining with unshed tears. 'You *are* enough.'

But the pressure to say what he should have said last night was overwhelming. He slid his hands down her bare arms and gripped her fingers. 'I know I'm a big risk for you, and I know that you're scared. I know that we wanted different things in the past, and that you've been hurt and let down before. I know that we can't afford to mess this up, because we're already a massive part of each other's lives. But I've half loved you for twenty years, Della. I was just too scared to fall all the way in case I discovered that there was, in fact, something unlovable about me. Something that meant you could never choose me.'

Della shook her head, tears landing on her cheeks. 'No, there isn't, and I do.'

'But I'm not scared anymore,' he said, only half hearing her as he cupped her face and wiped a tear away with the pad of his thumb. 'Well, that's not strictly true. I *am* scared. I'm terrified. But mainly about losing you, or having to live without you. So if you'll just give me a chance, one chance, at our relationship, I promise that I'll try and give you everything you've ever wanted. I'll try every day to be what you deserve. I'll never stop trying to make us work, because I'll always love you.'

Della laughed through her tears, throwing her arms around his neck. 'Harvey, you are already everything I want. You, us, the baby.'

'Really?' he asked, the lump in his throat so big he thought he might choke. But he was smart enough to grip her tight in case she changed her mind.

Della nodded, standing on her toes to press her lips to his. 'I'm sorry that I made you doubt yourself. It wasn't that you weren't enough. It was that *I* was still scared to trust my instincts and go after all of my dreams. But you showed me that I didn't have to settle, that I can have it all, as long as I follow my heart. And my heart leads to you, Harvey. I love you, too.'

Harvey held her close, his heart thudding wildly. 'Don't say it if you don't mean it,' he choked out, overcome. He was willing to hold on to her forever in the hopes that one day she might love him in return. As long as it took.

'I do mean it,' she cried, cupping his face. 'I want to move back to Melbourne and work with you, and raise our baby with you, and grow old with you, although I can't promise that we won't bicker from time to time.'

Harvey grinned, his heart soaring with hope. 'What's a little bit of harmless bickering when we're so good together in all other areas?' Before she could answer, he hauled her into his arms and slanted his lips over hers, kissing her with everything he was. Their tongues glided together, her fingers twisting his hair as her body shifted restlessly against his, seeking more.

Harvey pulled back, panting hard, her face gripped between his palms. 'You really love me?'

She leaned back and looked up at him, her emotions shining in her eyes. 'Of course I do. I almost told you last night, but then I thought you couldn't love me, and so I left first. I sabotaged this before you could hurt me, but I'm done being scared. I'm done putting my dreams on hold. I want us to build a life together. I want it all, and I know you can be everything I need, because you already are. I choose you, Harvey.'

Dragging her close again, Harvey kissed her until his head swam from lack of oxygen. 'Can we get out of here yet?' he asked, drying the rest of her tears. 'I want to take you home to bed before you fly back to New Zealand.'

Della laughed, rubbing at her smudged mascara. 'I think my brother might never speak to us again if we did that.'

Harvey shrugged, willing to risk it if she was, but they owed it to Jack to be present, not that the cute little fella would ever remember their sacrifice.

Della sobered, searching his stare. 'How do you feel...about the baby?' she asked with a frown of concern. 'I know it wasn't planned, and you're going from being alone to being in a relationship *and* being a father. That's a lot.'

His hands held her waist, but he wanted to drop to his knees and press a kiss to her stomach, where their baby grew. 'I feel like the luckiest man alive, Della. I love kids—tiny cute humans. I always have. They were just something else I denied myself because I was so used to holding back my emotions. But I don't know, something happened in Fiji. I kept seeing a different side to you and then another and then another, and I found myself helpless to letting you in. I found myself telling you things I've never told anyone else.'

She nodded. 'Me too.'

'But how are *you* feeling? Any morning sickness? You look a little tired?' Guilt for the way they'd left things last night crawled over his skin.

'I'm okay. I didn't sleep well last night,' she said, pressing her lips to his with a breathy sigh. 'But it's my own fault. I met this gorgeous man in Fiji and had the best sex of my life, the best holiday fling, and then I fell in love. But when I saw him again, I bottled it, despite being crazy about him, despite choosing him of all men.'

Harvey grinned, his ego inflating. 'The best sex, huh? Tell me more.'

Della rolled her eyes. 'Of course that's the thing you focus on.'

Laughing, he wrapped his arm around her shoulders and pressed a kiss to her temple as they headed back inside to the party. 'That first day in Fiji, you said it wasn't that great, so I'm just clarifying the details.'

Della nudged him with her elbow, tilting her face up for another kiss. 'Don't gloat.'

'I'm afraid you can't stop me.' He paused in the doorway and cupped her face, brushing his lips over hers.

When he pulled back, she looked up at him, slipping her arm around his waist, her other hand gripping his fingers on her shoulder. 'What will we tell them about us?'

She meant her family, the Wiltons, and Bill too, who'd been invited to join the celebration.

Harvey smiled, never more certain of anything in his life than he was about Della. 'We'll tell them the truth. We'll tell them I fell in love with you in Fiji.'

Della shook her head, that familiar spark of challenge he loved in her eyes. 'No, we'll tell them *I* fell in love with *you*.'

'Okay, you win.' He winked, chasing her lips with his in a final kiss before they pushed open the door to the restaurant and stepped into their future.

EPILOGUE

Two years later.

DELLA'S PAGER SOUNDED, summoning her to theatre. Her next patient must have left the surgical ward. She silenced the device, which was clipped to the pocket of her green Melbourne Medical Centre scrubs, and took the stairs. She was just about to turn the corner into the operating suites when Australia's hottest surgeon appeared in her path.

'Well, fancy meeting you here, Dr Wilton,' Harvey said, his stare travelling her body with a look that was way too indecent for the workplace.

'Are you following me again, Dr Ward?' she said, her breath trapped in her chest at how handsome he was and how, after almost two years of marriage, she was still crazy in love with him. 'Because you seem to be everywhere I look—in *my* bed, at *my* work, father to *my* children.' Pointedly, she glanced down at her pregnant belly, resting a hand over their growing son. 'If I didn't know you better, I'd guess you were my husband or something.'

They'd married in an intimate ceremony with family and friends four months before the birth of baby Lily, their daughter.

Harvey grinned, glanced along the corridor and then opened the nearest door, dragging Della into a utility room, the shelves of which were stacked with folded clean bed linens. 'Man, I missed you,' he said, hauling her as close as the baby bump would allow.

Della kissed him back, finally pulling back with a chuckle. 'Since this morning?'

'Yes,' he said simply, his expression sincere. That playful glint came into his eyes, doubling Della's pulse. 'Believe it or not, being married to you is the best thing that's ever happened to this old reformed bachelor. And the sex...' He rolled his eyes closed and groaned. 'Don't even get me started on how good that is. Some might say the best of their life...?'

Della laughed, too happy with his smug confidence to pull him up on his arrogance. When it came to accepting her love, trusting in it and giving her everything in return, her husband had risen to the top of the class during the past two years.

'I have to go,' she said, kissing him swiftly

once more. 'I have a man who came off his motorbike yesterday about to arrive in theatre.'

Harvey gripped her waist, blocking her escape. 'One more kiss to get me through the afternoon,' he begged, sliding his lips up the side of her neck so she shuddered against him with desire.

As she did every day, Della tangled her fingers in his hair and kissed him properly—her lips parting, her tongue sliding against his, her body shifting restlessly as she tried to manage how much he turned her on.

'Wow,' Harvey said when they parted, looking a little dazed. 'That was some kiss.'

'I'm softening you up,' she said, running her fingers through his hair in order to make him look presentable for his patients. 'Do you want day care pickup or dinner?'

Harvey groaned half-heartedly. 'Come on… I made dinner last night.'

'Perhaps you prefer both,' she said, playfully digging in her heels. 'My surgery will probably run over anyway.'

'Fine,' he said with a mock sigh, 'I suppose I'll pick up my adorable daughter from nursery and make my pregnant wife a delicious, nutritious meal for when she gets home from work.' Finally turning serious, he cupped her face and kissed her one last time. 'Leave it to me—the best sex and the best husband you've ever had.'

Della laughed, loving his competitive streak as much as she loved the rest of him. 'Don't forget the best father to our children,' she said, reaching for the door handle. Just before she left the glorified cupboard to sheepishly make her exit, hoping no one would see, she turned back. 'I love you.'

She never tired of saying that to Harvey. Nor had she ever grown used to the hint of bewilderment she saw in his eyes every time she did, as if he couldn't quite believe it was true.

'I love you too, Della.' He reached for her hand and squeezed her fingers. 'See you at home.'

She opened the door and was about to duck out when he pulled her back. His lips found hers, his hands gripping her face so tight, she forgot to breathe as he kissed her. When he pulled back, he rested his forehead against hers and whispered, 'Do you have everything that you've ever wanted?'

Dazed from the passion and desperation of his kiss and awash with love hormones, Della nodded, lost for words.

'Good,' Harvey said. 'Because that makes two of us.'

* * * * *

*If you enjoyed this story, check
out these other great reads
from JC Harroway*

Secretly Dating the Baby Doc
Nurse's Secret Royal Fling
Her Secret Valentine's Baby
Phoebe's Baby Bombshell

All available now!

HARLEQUIN
Reader Service

Enjoyed your book?

Try the perfect subscription for Romance readers and get more great books like this delivered right to your door.

See why over 10+ million readers have tried Harlequin Reader Service.

Start with a Free Welcome Collection with free books and a gift—valued over $20.

Choose any series in print or ebook. See website for details and order today:

TryReaderService.com/subscriptions